HEAVEN ON EARTH

SARA MADDERSON

Created with Vellum

For Chris, Paddy and Tilly.

1

It feels like the first day of school for Evelyn as much as for her eight-year-old son, Eddie. It's the first Monday in September, and in two hours' time Eddie will trot through the doors of his sweet new prep school, Knole Prep in Sevenoaks. After drop-off, Evelyn will head over to Sorrel Farm for her official first day as the farm and resort's new Commercial Director. She's been ramping up her knowledge of the place since accepting the role in July, but new staff are arriving today and she's looking forward to embracing the back-to-school vibe that September always brings. It's the perfect time of year to start her new adventure.

The hazy morning sunshine streams through the huge, east-facing bedroom windows in her brand-new home as she ends her yoga session and stretches out on the soft linens of her unmade bed with her mobile phone. She's had a few WhatsApps from Jess and Zoe overnight. Jess is Evelyn's oldest friend and took over the running of Sorrel Farm from her parents some years ago. She and her wife, Zoe, have transformed the farm into a fully organic producer and a chic resort. They struggled with the financial demands of such a venture until this summer, when a blessing dressed up as a crisis struck Evelyn.

Only four months ago, Evelyn's charmed life in London was shattered when her husband, the celebrity chef (and her business partner), Seb Macleod, was outed as gay by a tabloid. She fled down to Sorrel Farm with their son, Eddie, to find solace in its beautiful setting and in the company of her closest friends. While she and Seb navigated their way through the media storm that followed his coming out and unwound their marriage, she surprised herself by falling head over heels in love with Sorrel Farm's heavenly farm manager, Angus Rutherford. Angus is himself an old friend of Zoe's from Oxford and spearheads Jess and Zoe's efforts to transform the farm into a biodynamic haven.

It seemed as though she could have no future with Angus, given her considerable work commitments at Seb Macleod Limited. And then the solution fell into her lap. She resigned from her role as Marketing Director, stepped down from the board and sold her multi-million-pound stake in the business. She ploughed the majority of the proceeds into an equity stake in Sorrel Farm and agreed with Jess and Zoe that she would take on both business development and marketing for them.

The icing on the cake was her and Eddie's relocation from Holland Park to deepest Kent, which offered her the chance to build a new life and to be with Angus. On the same evening that Jess announced Evelyn's move to the press, Evelyn and Angus took their relationship to the next level. Since that magical night, things have moved at breakneck speed. A fortnight later, her property consultant found her this exquisite house. She and Eddie moved in last week; she offered the estate agent a considerable bump to his commission if he could get the sale closed before the start of the school year. And Angus has moved in too. His charming cottage near the farm is up for rent; he and Evelyn are determined to begin this new phase as they mean to go on: as a committed couple.

There's been a lot of change for Eddie to process. His father, Seb, has gone public with his relationship with Gino Donelli, Seb and Evelyn's former colleague. Angus is in Eddie's life now, as are his university-aged sons, Hector and Alistair, who live nearby with their mother during the holidays. Evelyn and Eddie spent a week in Devon with Angus and his boys in early August, growing closer and making new memories together.

Evelyn is in awe of how blithely Eddie is rolling with all these changes: the little guy seems to view everything that's happened as one big adventure, gaining father-figures and pseudo-brothers along the way. The biggest upshot where Eddie is concerned is that where Angus goes, his cocker-spaniel puppy, Charlie, follows. Eddie is devoted to Charlie, and the dog is already established in his room at night, despite Angus' protestations that a working dog belongs in the kitchen at best.

It's a relief that Eddie seems to be thriving amidst the upheaval—it's one less thing to consume her. Some days she can't quite believe how much she's taken on in one go: divorce, an exit from the company she helped to build, relocation to Kent, a new relationship, a new home, a new school for Eddie and, perhaps most intimidatingly of all, a new job.

The role at Sorrel Farm has come with a sizeable investment on her part, and a great deal of trust on the parts of Jess and Zoe. This is the baby of her oldest and dearest friends. It's a wonderful place. Its resort revives all who stay there, and its farm is en route to being an international poster-child for the virtues of biodynamics, if they give Angus the means to execute correctly. Her investment has shored up its balance sheet, but now the work begins to seize the huge opportunity before them. The stakes feel sky-high, but Evelyn being Evelyn, she matches every pang of fear with an adrenalin shot of exhilaration. Now the fun will begin. She can't wait to see what they can do with this little piece of heaven.

As she shifts on her stomach, luxuriating on the white cloud of duvet beneath her, the door opens. It's Angus, balancing a small tray with two coffee mugs on the outstretched fingers of one hand as he shuts the door with the other. She beams at him.

'You made it back! I wasn't sure you would.'

He puts the tray on the bedside table and sits on the bed, shooting her a grin so delicious, so hungry, that she's not sure her body will ever stop responding to it.

'And miss the chance to see you in my favourite outfit? Not likely.'

He runs a hand down over her crop top and the bare small of her back, and over the curve of her bum. The friction of his calloused skin lights up her nerve-endings, and her skin hums. She shifts onto one elbow and reaches for him with her other hand, tracing a line over his eyebrow, down his cheek, along his jawbone, and down his neck to the V of his shirt collar. He bends his head to one side and nuzzles into her palm as it cradles him.

'How were the morning rounds at the farm?'

'Fine.' He yawns. 'Pretty quiet. I can't believe I won't have to set my alarm for four-thirty anymore from next week.'

One of the first things Evelyn did after investing was to request that their Finance Director, Ned, allocate budget to hire someone experienced to work under Angus. Not only has Angus been too caught up in the day-to-day, often reactive, running of the farm to devote himself fully to the big strategic issues, but she plans to work him far too hard in bed at night for him to cope with a four-thirty start every weekday morning. This new hire will be the best money she's spent.

'I can't wait,' she says. 'But you hope you're not expecting to get any extra sleep under the new schedule? I have big plans for you.'

He bends his head to hers. 'I'll be hugely disappointed if I get any sleep at all,' he says, and kisses her. His lips are soft and his stubble sandpapery; he hasn't shaved yet this morning. She inhales the smell of his skin greedily.

'But leaving you in bed and sneaking out in the dark is the absolute worst,' he continues. 'I can't wait to wake up with you every morning. Now, do you need a shower? Can I help you with that?' He kisses her again and runs a hand down the front of the crop top, his thumb lightly skimming her nipple through the fabric. She shudders as a bolt of electricity flashes down her abdomen, and opens her mouth slightly to let him know how much she appreciates his touch.

'Do you have time?' she mumbles against his lips. 'Don't you have to get back to the farm?'

'Nope,' he says. His finger has now worked its way beneath the elasticated bottom of her crop top and is stroking the underside of her left breast. 'I've told the new guy—Danny—to report for duty at nine. There wasn't any reason to hang around at the farm. I can even go with you to drop Eddie if you like, to get the lay of the land? And besides, I'd like to help you out of this thing, just because I can. I don't think the novelty of undressing you will ever wear off, sweetheart.'

She laughs and leans into him. Her yoga outfit has become a highly charged joke between them. She was wearing it the first time she met Angus at the farm—she was doing a vinyasa flow on the front lawn of her little holiday cottage early one May morning, when Charlie scampered over and assaulted her face during a headstand. On the night he found out she'd be staying in Kent permanently and they had the means to make a go of things together, Angus confessed to her that he'd been fantasising about peeling the top off her ever since that first encounter. In the intervening weeks he's shown remarkable enthusiasm every time she's worn her yoga gear. She prides herself on having an impressive designer wardrobe, but this little top is a red rag to a bull where he's concerned.

'Is Eddie awake yet?' she asks.

'I peeked in. He's still out cold and Charlie's downstairs.'

She looks at her phone. Six-fifteen. They have over an hour and a half until they need to leave for the school run. She can definitely squeeze in a steamy shower session with her irresistible boyfriend. He's wearing his standard weekday uniform of a Sorrel Farm gilet and checked shirt, open at the neck and rolled up to the elbows, revealing forearms so tanned and muscular that they got her pulse racing from that very first meeting. She pushes herself up onto her knees, holds her arms over her head and raises her eyebrows at him.

'Go on then, gorgeous. Knock yourself out.'

He grins and grips the sides of her top, easing it up over her sensitised breasts and her head. She shakes out her hair.

'Jesus,' he says, his eyes devouring her. 'I am such a lucky bastard.'

A COUPLE OF HOURS LATER, they pull up not far from the school gates. Angus is gratified that the radiant smile he put on her face during their shower session hasn't yet faded. He's even more gratified that he alone knows the reason for that smile, and for the particular bounce in her step that morning. Otherwise, she's her usual, immaculate self, courting the warm September sunshine in huge shades and a long, floaty dress that skims her incredible body. He stifles a grin. She's still determined to dress as though she's on Bond Street rather than about to spend the day on a farm. Not that he's complaining. She looks sensational. At least she's learnt to wear flats.

She holds Eddie's hand and the boy skips along beside her, looking dapper in his brand-new navy and green school uniform. Angus walks behind them, not a little emotional. His joy at finding love with Evelyn is still so close to the surface, and being able to relive the wonders of childhood through little Eddie is a gift he hadn't realised he wanted so badly. He hasn't done a school drop-off for years. They turn into the school gates, past a snake of cars that moves painfully slowly up the driveway.

'Goodness,' Evelyn says, 'I'm so pleased the head-mistress tipped us off about parking outside if we wanted to do a proper drop-off. This traffic is worse than Notting Hill was!'

Other parents and children are also streaming up the path, and Angus clocks curious glances at Evelyn from parents coming in the opposite direction, as well as some jolts of recognition. It hasn't been long since she and Seb were splashed across every news outlet in the English-speaking world. She seems not to notice the looks. He hopes she'll find respite here. It's only twenty miles from London as the crew flies but she's out of the melting-pot now, and he hopes very much that she and Eddie can enjoy a new, less frantic pace of life here. That he can play a part in their future happiness makes his cup run over.

He knows he wants to marry her. He's known it on some level from the early days of her stay at the farm. This hasn't been a normal relationship, where tentative texting and semi-regular dates define the initial stage. The night of the party that showcased Sorrel Farm to the press and announced Evelyn's involvement, he and she finally found a path forward as a proper couple, and their relationship immediately escalated to 'on' status. No messing about. No dragging their feet. They told Eddie almost immediately and carted him off to Devon with Angus' boys for some bonding time. The following week he and she escaped to the south of France for a few much-needed days alone and he told her he loved her, and that he saw his entire future with her. Thankfully, she said the same.

So, when Evelyn's offer on Belvedere, her beautiful new home in Kent, was accepted, she made it clear she wanted Angus to move in with her and Eddie.

'I know it's fast,' she said. 'But it's the perfect opportunity to build a new life together. This house will be as new to me as it will be to you. No one's having to make a home for themselves on anyone else's turf. It's neutral territory—a fresh start.'

It's also palatial. He has no financial concerns thanks to a large trust fund (though his elder brother had inherited the vast family estate in Derbyshire), but the wealth Evelyn and her husband have accumulated is on a different level. Their divorce is ticking along amicably and efficiently, and the sale of their villa in Holland Park is in progress for the princely sum of twenty-nine million. He's been up there with her a couple of times over the summer to help her organise the necessary logistics. It's awe-inspiring: interior-designed with hand-painted wallpapers that even he can appreciate, and featuring a subterranean gym. It was clear that a chintzy cottage in Kent wouldn't cut it for Evelyn.

Belvedere, the house they've chosen as the canvas upon which to paint a new life together, is perfect. It's an old, square Georgian manor in Ightham, halfway between the Bourne Valley where Sorrel Farm nestles and Eddie's new Sevenoaks school. Gnarled wisteria winds around the pillars of the doorway and will be a vision come May. It has a pool and tennis court, both of which should keep Eddie and his friends happy for years to come, but Evelyn was sold on the magical little walled kitchen garden. Angus can't wait to get his hands on it properly—they only got the keys a week ago.

Like Evelyn, he has big plans for their life together in this house. He won't freak her out yet, but he sees a baby brother or sister for Eddie tottering around on the lawns. All in good time. She has to finalise her divorce first.

They hug Eddie goodbye and hand him over to the young, smiley headmistress. Angus takes Evelyn's hand.

'Right,' he says. 'Let's get you off to *your* first proper day at school.'

She squeezes his hand. 'Bring it on.'

2

The mere act of following the long driveway up to Sorrel Farm is enough to slow Sadie's heart rate. She did a trial run of the drive in her new, leased Mini Cooper last week, shortly after she moved down to Sevenoaks. The farm is accessed via endless country lanes that all look the same, so she wanted to be sure she had the route down pat and wouldn't be completely beholden to Waze on her all-important first day.

As she drives up the driveway, she kills the radio. Gravel scrunches underfoot and the swaying canopy of green overhead gives voice to birdsong. It sounds as if there is an actual orchestra of birds up there, in contrast to the incessant cooing of pigeons in London. All her senses are heightened. This is laughably contrary to her experience of arriving at the *Tribune* every day for the past eight years. Gone is the mad daily squash on the Northern Line from Balham to Waterloo, and the head-down battle with thousands of fellow commuters for pavement and escalator space. Gone too is that swell of awe and pride that always hit her when she pushed through the rotating doors into the *Tribune*'s vast marble lobby with its unique smell. The paper hasn't occupied real estate on Fleet Street for decades, and yet the scent of power lingered in that lobby.

She always showed up for work believing that she could make a real difference, that she had a voice and a responsibility. She isn't naïve, but the *Tribune* was pretty good at force-feeding its own Kool-Aid to its employees. For years, the career path ahead was straight as an arrow; all she had to do was keep her head down, her blinkers on and her feet moving forward, one piece of journalism at a time.

And now she's thrown all that away—the adrenalin rush, the opportunities, the glamour, the *access*—to go in-house and help build the Sorrel Farm brand from the ground up. It's utterly left-field, and her ex-colleagues and friends thought she was bananas to walk away from the *Tribune* just as her star was in the ascendant. She can't quite explain the madness that took hold of her a few weeks ago when she asked Evelyn to consider her if a role came up at the farm.

She was dazzled by Evelyn, of course. It was impossible not to be. She wore such an aura of success and wealth, but she wore it lightly, with grace and humour. Sadie first encountered her on the rooftop of private members' club White City House, hiding pool-side the day Seb Macleod came out as gay to the *Post*. Evelyn wasn't too happy to be approached by a journalist then, but she invited Sadie down to Sorrel Farm for the press event at which she announced her new role and investment, and the magic of it all reeled Sadie in. The place entrances her; it's stunning and restorative and other-worldly. And the fact that a businessperson as shrewd and established as Evelyn Macleod has seen enough potential in it to walk away from her eight-figure empire and pile millions of pounds worth of capital into it is the only endorsement Sadie needs to believe in the possibilities Sorrel Farm offers.

There was something in the air that night: the resort enchanted all the journalists and influencers who came along to the alfresco dinner in the walled garden. They ate produce fresh from the land around them and were bewitched by Evelyn's infectious energy and the passion of owners Jess and Zoe. It was apparent to all the guests that this hidden gem was on the cusp of going stratospheric. Sadie pitched a glowing comeback piece on Evelyn for the *Tribune*'s Sunday supplement and shot her for the cover in the walled garden. It was the easiest pitch she'd ever made to her editors and Evelyn called her a couple of days after it hit the newsstands, asking her to head up their PR efforts at the farm.

The scope of her new role is undeniably exciting. Evelyn has bitten off a great deal: Commercial Director as well as Chief Marketing Officer. From their phone conversations, Sadie knows how invaluable Evelyn will be to leveraging the Sorrel Farm brand—she performed the same alchemy on her ex-husband's eponymous empire. She also has so many opportunities to consider on the business development side, from expanding the farm's production capacity to establishing the resort as one of the UK's top foodie havens. She'll be pulled in so different directions and she'll need a solid marketing team below her.

This is where Sadie comes in. As a seasoned journalist, she's perfectly placed to build a rapport with the press, and as a thirty-year-old woman recently out of a five-year relationship, she's itching for a change of scene. Not that moving to Kent is a particularly smart move if she wants some action. Are there even single men in Kent? Or is everyone married and living smugly with their glossy wives and privately educated children behind large gates? But even a few weeks of trying her luck on Bumble in London has left her exhausted and disillusioned. Perhaps abstinence is the answer. Abstinence, and a new role that will consume all her energy.

Remembering Evelyn's instructions, she continues down the driveway past signs that read Cottages, Oast House and Walled Garden until she sees a sign for Staff. Just ahead lies the staff carpark, and she finds a spot before crunching over the gravel on foot to the Oast House to meet Evelyn for their nine o'clock coffee. She spent a night down here for the press event and didn't want to leave. It's surreal to regard everything through the lens of someone who's now a part of this community as opposed to a fleeting visitor. Perhaps it'll lose some of its magic once she sees behind the scenes. She suspects the opposite is true: she'll grow to love it more than she already does.

THE OAST HOUSE IS BUZZING. A quick glance around the space identifies likely hotel guests, clusters of well-groomed women in tennis gear or school-run outfits, and a handful of people on their laptops—probably local entrepreneurs. It's a huge, airy space with vaulted ceilings and a mezzanine at either end. In front of the open kitchen stands a long trestle table laden with delicious-looking food. She only had a coffee before leaving the flat, and her stomach rumbles at the sight of the spread.

As she looks around for a table, Evelyn enters and approaches her, smiling and waving. She has on a floral maxi-dress that Sadie instantly clocks as current-season Chloé. She looks immaculate.

'Hey!' Evelyn throws her arms around Sadie. 'The cavalry is here! I'm so happy to see you!'

Sadie laughs and kisses her on both cheeks. As at their previous encounters, Evelyn's energy and enthusiasm are infectious.

'This beats rush-hour London, that's for sure.' She takes a seat as Evelyn does the same.

'Doesn't it? I can't believe this is our new office.' Evelyn gestures at the picturesque courtyard outside with her hand. 'I'm glad we're both starting on the same day—makes it less scary.'

'Definitely,' Sadie says. Evelyn doesn't seem like the type of boss she needs to put up a facade with. Nevertheless, she says, 'I'm very excited about being a part of the team. Thanks for taking a punt on me.'

'It wasn't much of a punt. We're lucky to have you. You know how the game is played. Have you found yourself somewhere to live?'

'Yeah. In Sevenoaks. I'm renting a bedroom from a couple with a flat—I found it on Gumtree. It's not hugely exciting, but it's roomy and has a parking space. It'll do for now.'

'Good,' Evelyn says. 'I've just completed on my new house too—we got the keys last week. It's been a crazy few weeks but I'm thrilled to be in.'

'Congratulations. Just you and your son, right?'

'Eddie, yes.' Evelyn hesitates. 'I should get you up to speed on something. Remember Angus Rutherford—the farm manager here?'

'Of course.' Sadie conducted a phone interview with Angus to clarify some production facts for her article on Evelyn and Sorrel Farm.

'Well, Angus and I are together. We got together the

night of the press dinner, actually.' Evelyn blushes and plays with her napkin.

'Wow!' Sadie stares. 'I had no idea! Good for you—you deserve it, after all you've been through with Seb. Is it serious?'

'Very,' Evelyn says. 'He's moved in to the new house—we're making a fresh start together.'

'Jesus,' Sadie says. 'I'm looking forward to meeting him—he must be pretty special if you've already shacked up with him.'

'He is.' Evelyn is dreamy. 'He's amazing. I thought we could grab a bite to eat here and then go for a walk around the farm. It's more fun to walk and chat than to do it at a desk, and it'll give you a better picture of all the moving parts—you can look at it all through a press lens. With any luck, we'll run into Angus and you can meet him properly. He's excited to meet you—I've been raving about you. It's going to be a lot of fun, Sadie. We're going to do great things together.'

AFTER A MUCH-NEEDED breakfast of obscenely tasty granola, laden with toasted nuts and honey, Sadie follows Evelyn out into the courtyard. Guests and members lounge beneath umbrellas on low outdoor sofas, and late summer flowers pour out of wooden wheelbarrows. Along the edge of the Oast House stand wooden crates stamped *Sorrel Farm,* heavy with herbs. The overall effect is magical. She hopes it won't lure her into a stupor of indulgent rosé-drinking. She's here to work.

Evelyn gives her a swift refresh of the heart of the resort, talking as they walk. They pass through the idyllic walled garden, home to the press party and the location for the *Tribune* shoot, as Evelyn summarises the breadth of the kitchen garden offering, the extent to which it informs the menu at the Oast House, and the opportunities for supplying more restaurants and catering companies now Seb Macleod Ltd is on board as a major client.

'It's relatively easy to ramp up production here, apparently,' Evelyn tells her. 'There's an overflow kitchen garden next door which is massive, and Angus is working on extending our population of laying hens because Seb wants to get his hands on as many of our eggs as he can for their corporate events and his Westbourne Grove restaurant.'

They stroll between the large raised beds of leaves and shoots. Sadie would struggle to identify most of the vegetables without the labelled stakes next to them.

'It should be an exciting time to be here,' Evelyn continues. 'We'll celebrate the harvest festival in a month; it'll be a chance to get some foodie press down to the farm.'

'You mentioned plans for a cookbook of some sort, last time we spoke?'

Evelyn grins. 'Yes. I'm very excited about that. We've got a meeting about it later with the publisher—you should definitely sit in on it.'

'You have a publisher already? I didn't realise you were that far along.'

'She's Seb's publisher,' Evelyn clarifies. 'She published *Honest Food* and most of his previous ones, so we've known her for years. We don't have the content completely agreed upon yet; she's coming to work on that with us today. But realistically it will be a year before it's published, so that gives you a good lead-time to build some great press relationships.'

'What's the angle of the book?' Sadie asks.

'That's what we're discussing today.' Evelyn grimaces. 'You remember Zoe, our head chef, from the party?'

'Jess' wife? Yes, she's hard to forget. She's absolutely stunning.'

'Exactly. She'll make the most amazing face of Sorrel Farm as far as its gastronomic offering goes. But she's shy, and self-effacing—she couldn't be less interested in having a public profile. We can pitch the book as a gorgeous seasonal bible, with food-porn galore, but centring it around Zoe will be what puts this place on the map, you mark my words.'

3

As they leave the walled garden, Evelyn checks her phone.

'Angus is back at the office, apparently. He has a new starter today too; he's filling out some paperwork. Let's head back there and we can get you introduced to everyone.'

'Which teams work from there?'

'Mainly management and support staff. It's an informal layout—you'll see. Jess is there most of the time—she's basically our COO; Zoe's based in the kitchen, but she comes in to work on procurement and financials with our Finance Director, Ned—he's amazing. I couldn't have got my investment in this place sorted so quickly without him pulling all-nighters. He has a couple of bookkeepers working for him. Then there's our assistant and office manager, Lauren, who's a lot of fun.

'The hospitality staff are based out of the Oast House and Angus comes in to work on budgets and expenses with Jess and Ned, but he's in the field as much as possible—he hates being desk-based. All the customer services for the resort are handled remotely by ZenDesk. The plan over the next year is to hire more heavily, especially for sales and marketing, so you should see the place fill up over the next few months. I'll likely float around between the office and the resort and I'm intending to be up in London at least once a week, schmoozing where it makes sense.'

'Got it,' Sadie says as Evelyn pushes open the door of a barn conversion by the staff carpark. The space they walk into is large and airy, with vaulted ceilings and light wooden beams—a far cry from the artificially lit, carpet-tiled *Tribune* offices. It's laid out for hot-desking; ergonomic chairs flank the huge, glossy white tables and the people sitting at them are mainly on laptops. It smells comfortingly of coffee and toast.

'Morning, Lauren,' Evelyn says, swinging her huge Goyard tote off her shoulder and onto the floor by the nearest table. 'Meet Sadie, our new head of PR.'

A twenty-something woman rises from her chair. Her dark hair is centre-parted and tonged in long waves, and her face is immaculately made up and contoured. Her beauty regime is definitely Kardashian-based: her false eyelashes are dense and she's had her lips filled. She's in spray-on jeans, plasticky heels and a milkmaid-style top. She looks exactly like most of the support staff at the paper. But the smile she directs at Sadie is genuine. She likely knows how to have fun.

'All right, Sadie?' she asks. 'Welcome to the farm!'

She looks even less likely than Sadie to be based on a working farm. At least they aren't all going to be ruddy farmer-types.

A man walks towards them, grinning at Evelyn as if he's

just run a *marathon de sable* and she's a bottle of Lucozade. So this is Angus. He's hot. Old—he must be mid-forties—but hot. He wraps an arm around her waist and kisses her hair, and she melts into him. Wow. So they definitely aren't keeping this on the down-low at work.

'Sadie,' Evelyn says, breaking away and beaming at him, 'meet Angus.'

'Thank you for coming to rescue Evelyn,' he says, turning his grin on her. 'She's been so excited to have you on board.'

He's definitely sexy. Well done, Evelyn—not that she isn't a total catch too. But it must be fun for her to have this hot guy worshipping at her feet, after having had a secretly gay husband for who knows how long.

'I'm excited too,' she says. To have Evelyn's enthusiasm for her arrival confirmed by a third party is a welcome boost.

'I have a new team member starting today too—my Assistant Farm Manager,' Angus says. 'We've just been getting him set up.' He turns and beckons. 'Danny. Over here.'

A guy stands up from the far table and strolls towards them. Holy shit. He's ridiculous. His short, dark-blonde hair is tousled and his white Sorrel Farm polo shirt and beige shorts showcase a fantastic tan. He's clearly been working outside all summer. She wonders if it's a builder's tan or if it continues underneath that shirt. She wouldn't mind finding out. She hasn't considered that the farm workers might be such an attractive bunch, but it makes total sense they would be. All that toiling in fields day after day... she stands a little taller.

As Angus introduces them, Danny runs his eyes

unapologetically up and down her body before flashing her a dazzling grin and offering his hand.

'Hi there,' he says in a posh accent. Public school boy, probably. But right now she doesn't care what his voice is like. She takes his hand; it's warm and strong.

'Sadie Thomas,' she says crisply in her most proper London voice. His grin doesn't falter. Her *froideur* doesn't fool him for a minute; she can tell.

'Evelyn may be happy to have you on board, Sadie,' Angus says, 'but let me tell you, Danny's going to change my life. From next week he'll be taking over the morning rounds for me, so he'll be the poor bugger getting up at four-thirty while I slumber.'

'Don't remind me,' Danny groans, rubbing the back of his neck with a tanned hand. She tries not to watch.

'I'm as grateful as Angus is,' Evelyn says. 'Maybe we can start staying up past nine o'clock.' She strokes Angus' arm affectionately.

Danny winks at Evelyn. 'I can see why he wants to have a lie-in with you. I'd be exactly the same, in his place.'

'You can cut that out right now, if you want to last longer than a day in this job,' Angus says good-naturedly.

Sadie tries not to roll her eyes. It's no mystery what kind of guy he is. The problem is, he probably gets away with hitting on everyone because he's so bloody attractive.

'Drinks at five,' Evelyn says, 'in the Oast House, to welcome the new team members and toast the start of the apple harvest. I hope you guys can make it.'

Danny's eyes are on Sadie's face. They're very blue against his tan. She holds eye contact and raises her eyebrows at him challengingly.

'I'll see *you* at the bar,' he says to her.

Oh, shit.

NED IS WORKING on the management accounts for the resort side of the business. He's been in the office for a couple of hours already, and he's fully in the zone, playing around with the inputs on his spreadsheet and delighting in the instant cascade of fresh data whenever he changes an input. Voices break his concentration despite the classical music playing through his AirPods, and he looks over towards the entrance.

There's Evelyn, Angus and some other guy. Someone else is standing beside Evelyn, but the guys are blocking his view. He's a big fan of both Evelyn and Angus. Angus he's known for a couple of years, since he moved back to Kent and took up the FD role. Ned rates him highly; he's extremely smart and a straight-talker. They communicate easily and Angus always strikes him as a supremely competent captain of the ship that is the farm. God knows, they've had some storms, navigating seas of red on their balance sheet and profit-and-loss statements over the past couple of years. Through them all, Angus has been rational and realistic. He makes Ned's job easier.

That the seas of red are now black is one reason he's warmed to Evelyn so quickly. Over the summer, he spent an intensive week with Evelyn and Jess, running the numbers every which way and arriving at a valuation that reflected the potential of the farm while providing an attractive entry-point for Evelyn as an investor. He was gratified by her financial literacy and her ability to absorb large gluts of data. She now has a thirty percent equity stake in The Sorrel Farm Group, the entity that covers both the farming and resort businesses.

If Angus has made Ned's job easier, Evelyn's arrival and

her cash injection have made it a joy. Instantly, the question mark over the survival of the farm has been removed. His first two years, he had the excruciating responsibility of improving their cash flow wherever he could—holding off payments to suppliers and placating the bank, the size of whose credit line made Ned and the bank equally nervous. Now, there's cash in the coffers and the feeling of endless possibility in the air, thanks to Evelyn's arrival and her incredible energy and connections. Instead of survival, he can sink his teeth indulgently into helping Jess, Zoe, Angus and Evelyn maximise the potential of this little gem.

His eyes and focus return to the numbers in front of him. He's rebuilding all their financial models from the ground up, and he'll need a lot of time with the management team this autumn to forecast all the capital expenditure, or CapEx, they want to implement with their new nest-egg. He pushes some strands of hair off his face with one hand while the other hovers over a cell on his spreadsheet with the track pad—is he happy with that CapEx assumption as a percentage of sales?

His peripheral vision notes a swishing movement, and he looks up to find Evelyn standing over him. As usual, she looks as though she's stepped out of the pages of some fashion magazine. He was pleasantly surprised by how friendly and down to earth she was when he first met her. She and Angus are far better suited than they may seem to anyone who doesn't know them. Now she gives him a radiant smile.

'Morning, Ned! Sorry to disturb you. I'd like to introduce you to our new PR manager, Sadie Thomas. She's starting today, and she'll be working closely with me to build the farm's profile in the press.'

A woman steps out from behind Evelyn, and the

muscles in his jaw and neck tighten. He exhales sharply through his nose. His first impression is of sunshine: golden skin, light golden hair scraped back with shades perched jauntily on top. She has on a short, belted dress that buttons all the way down the front and exposes a narrow V of sun-kissed chest. He doesn't know much about women's fashion but this looks kind of military: it's beige—or khaki? Long, bare, golden legs. She's a few years younger than him—likely late twenties.

He stands up, smooths down his chinos and blinks; his contact lenses always stick when he stares at a screen for too long. He holds out his hand.

'Welcome, Sadie. It's good to meet you. I'm Ned Fitzsimmons; I'm the Finance Director here.'

'How do you do,' she says disinterestedly. She looks right through him—he could swear that if someone were to show her a photo of him in a line-up a few hours later, she'd claim she'd never met him. Up close, her eyes are extraordinary—pale aqua, ringed with darker blue and very white whites, and fringed with thick lashes. Her nose turns up slightly at the end—it's adorable—and across it lies a perfect smattering of freckles. Beneath the freckles, her skin is dewy and perfect. She doesn't seem to be wearing much makeup, but you can never tell.

'I'm sure you guys will have some interaction when we need to go through PR budgets,' Evelyn says. 'We'll be ramping our events up substantially this season.'

He tears his gaze away from Sadie's face to Evelyn's. 'Righto,' he says. God. He sounds like he's walked straight out of a PG Wodehouse novel.

Sadie makes no comment.

'See you at drinks this evening?' Evelyn asks, as they make to walk on.

'Of course,' he says, and stands back as Sadie stalks past him without a word. She's captivating. Pity she's so lacking in charm. She obviously isn't remotely bothered about making connections on her first day. He shakes his head as he sits down and tries to remember what it was about his CapEx forecasts he found so enthralling a minute earlier.

4

The lunchtime rush is over, and afternoon sunlight streams through the glass doors of the Oast House. The vast room is relatively quiet, but the light catches the dust particles and transforms the stillness into a swirling, dancing spectacle before Evelyn's eyes as she and Sadie mount the stairs to the mezzanine level, where a large oval table is already populated with women. Among them is the Penguin editor, Avery: a glossy-looking suited brunette.

Opposite her sits Clara, the photographer she's has had on Zoe's tail ever since she conceived of a Sorrel Farm cook book, and with whom Zoe has thankfully forged an instant connection. Clara is a mum from Zoe and Jess' kids' school, and Jess suggested her as an option when Evelyn expressed her desire to start shooting seasonal footage as soon as possible. While it's helpful to have a local to tail Zoe, the idea of plucking a mum from Jess' school network sounded amateurish until Evelyn saw Clara's delightful, sensual photography and was instantly captivated. She's proven a wonderful hire, in part because she and Zoe hit it off so well. Evelyn senses that Clara has the same artistic dreaminess that Zoe does; her head often seems in the clouds and the two appear to have discovered a like-minded soul in each other.

Introductions made, she dives in. 'Avery is here because we've agreed in principle that a cookbook based on Sorrel Farm's farming and food philosophy is interesting.'

Avery nods her agreement.

She continues, 'There's a strong argument for dividing the book up by seasons, because seasonal eating is the optimal way to eat for our health and that of the planet. But of course that requires a full year of gathering footage and content. That's why I hired Clara as soon as I knew I'd be joining the farm; I wanted us to get started with the photography ASAP.'

'What are you focusing your photography on?' Avery asks.

Clara consults her notebook. She's an exceptionally pretty, curvy brunette with a voice so soft that Evelyn leans forward to listen when she speaks. 'Evelyn gave me six mandates: seasonal landscapes and nature; the workings of the farm; the produce itself; plated or styled meals; tablescapes or seasonal displays; and Zoe and her team in the kitchen.'

'And are you getting what you need?' Evelyn asks.

'Mostly, yes. I've got tonnes of footage of the farm over the summer, the straw harvest, the orchards in the last few weeks, the herds. And I take photos of the produce both growing and in the kitchen.' She looks at Zoe for confirmation.

'The missing element, so far, is the dishes themselves,'

Zoe says, 'precisely because we have not finalised the exact recipes we want to include in the book. But Clara reads through our menus for the week ahead every Monday, and she and I decide in advance which seasonal plates she will come to photograph. Then she takes images of us preparing those meals too.'

'That's ok.' Avery tucks a sleek strand of hair behind her ear. 'We can recreate dishes after the fact, using imported produce and a food stylist, should we need to. Are you using a food stylist right now?'

Zoe and Evelyn exchange a glance.

'Not right now,' Evelyn says. 'I realise we may need to use one to fill in any missing dishes, as you say. But Zoe has a unique and beautiful presentation style—it's very organic. She uses edible flowers and foraged produce to decorate her dishes, and we're keen to stick as closely to that look as possible for the recipe pages. We'll need a stylist for the tablescapes, but we use an event planner—Siobhan Quinn—for our seasonal events and I suggest we capture as much content as possible in situ at those events. Our next one will be the Harvest Festival early next month.'

'Agreed.' Avery scribbles something in her notebook. 'What I'd like to do today is confirm the overall philosophy of the book, beyond simply seasonality, and once that's done we can put together a starting list of recipes to showcase that philosophy.'

Evelyn nods at Zoe. There's only one person who can articulate the full potential magic of this book, but Zoe's made it clear, albeit in her own diplomatic way, that she's deeply reluctant to put her face to this endeavour. Right now, she's on board with a Sorrel Farm cook book but not a Zoe Augustin one. They have a road to climb; Evelyn knows

Avery won't rest until they have Zoe on the cover. 'Over to you, my dear.'

Zoe takes a breath. Even in her chef's whites, her beauty is otherworldly. Sadie and Avery both stare at her as she begins to speak.

'For me, it's what we call *la communion*,' she says, leaning forward, hands outstretched on the table, palms up. 'It's the same in English. When we plant, and when we nurture our produce and the soil that nourishes it, and then when we take that produce and put it in our bodies... all that is a sacred pact with the land. We are communing with nature through these acts, and for me it's one of the most spiritual practices we can perform. It's a privilege. And when we respect nature, and its plants and animals, and then the food that nature gives us nourishes our bodies and our souls, there's a perfect—*symbiose.* Symbiosis. For me and the team here, this is the only kind of philosophy, of relationship, we can contemplate having with the land and with our food.'

There's silence when she finishes.

'Goosebump moment,' Avery says, crossing her bare arms and rubbing them. She glances at Evelyn, opens her mouth and hesitates.

'I agree that this idea of communion is a compelling launchpad for putting your philosophy down on paper. In fact, *Communion* would make a wonderful title for the book.'

Excellent. In her mind, Evelyn pounds the table. 'I'm so glad you said that.' She's grinning. 'I thought the same, but naturally you guys have the ultimate naming rights. Still, if we have that word in our mind as the title it will really allow us to build the book around that concept.'

'I think that would be very powerful,' Avery says. 'And... I've made my views on this clear to Evelyn, but listening to you speak, Zoe, has clarified them further: I absolutely believe you should be the spokesperson for communicating this ideology in the book. You're articulate and passionate, I can already tell you have lashings of integrity, and you have an allure, for want of a better word, that will come off the page. I really believe you will draw people into your world, not just by how you look—you're obviously an incredibly beautiful woman—but through the magic of your personality. Without you as the explicit voice—and face—the book will be just another cookbook.'

She sits back and crosses her arms, her eyes searching Zoe's face for a sign of acquiescence. Zoe sits silently, her breathing slow and even. She looks outwardly serene, but Evelyn's known her long enough to sense something's up. She'll get to the bottom of it eventually, but meanwhile her job is to ensure Avery has fallen sufficiently in love with Zoe that she offers them a publishing contract, and to ensure Zoe gets so sucked in by the importance of sharing her food philosophy far and wide that she'll see compromising her privacy as an acceptable price to pay.

'Zoe's a passionate evangelist when it comes to waking society up to the perils of our current eating habits and the benefits of adopting a more sustainable approach to food,' she tells Avery now. She raises her eyebrows at Zoe, who responds feebly.

'For sure.'

'I'm sure you'll find the entire Sorrel Farm team views this proposed book as a crucial part of spreading our message,' Evelyn says firmly. 'And we're all willing to do what's necessary to give this book the platform it deserves.' She's bulldozing Zoe; it's not how she wanted to play this, but she'll deal with that later. Having got Avery down to the farm for a precious couple of hours, she intends to gain as much momentum on closing this deal as possible. She wants a contract, and if Avery needs reassurance that Zoe will front the book, that's what she'll get. She avoids eye contact with Zoe and focuses her attention on Avery. 'Shall we discuss what kind of structure you think would work for the book?'

5

Sadie is exhausted by the time five o'clock rolls around and they're due for drinks in the Oast House. The strain of absorbing endless amounts of new information is making itself felt. The meeting about Zoe's cookbook was a highlight. It's gratifying to be privy to the discussions at such an early stage; it bodes well for her ability to get under the skin of Sorrel Farm's food offering and pitch its unique value to the press.

Zoe herself also fascinates her. She's astonishingly beautiful, with her light hazel eyes and olive skin, but Sadie suspects there's no ego at play. If there was, she'd surely jump at the chance to be the star of the book. There's something funny going on there. Zoe strikes her as otherworldly. She can't imagine her stressing or flapping, in the kitchen or elsewhere. And yet, Sadie observed her during and after her short, moving speech. When Avery was addressing Zoe, she could swear she looked like a hunted animal. Odd.

The last hour of the afternoon has passed uneventfully. She's started a master spreadsheet of press contacts for the farm. There are so many angles through which they can court the press: the ongoing shift to a fully biodynamic way of farming, the farm-to-table eating, the colourful characters in the team, Evelyn's arrival and, of course, the magic of the resort side. The hotel and facilities manage to be world class and utterly authentic at the same time. The biggest risk, in her view, is ensuring it doesn't become a victim of its own success.

On the dot of five, Lauren grabs her and drags her to the loos where Sadie combs her chin-length hair back into its customary short ponytail and applies a dab of apricot lip gloss and a dusting of bronzer. Her Ibiza tan is holding up well. She watches in amusement as Lauren lays on the lipliner, gloss, powder and mascara with a trowel. She finishes the effect with far too much perfume. Her hair hasn't moved at all, but Lauren peppers her head with hairspray for good measure.

As they stroll through the resort to the Oast House, Lauren chatters away.

'My boyfriend, Tom, works with Angus on the farm,' she confides.

'Did you meet him here?'

Lauren nods happily. 'Yes, and we've been going out for two years; we live together in Plaxtol, not far from here. He loves working with Angus.'

'I met Angus earlier, with some new guy who was so fucking hot, I thought I was hallucinating. Danny, I think?'

'Yes, I met him earlier, too. He's absolutely lush, isn't he? I'll have to get the dirt on him from Tom. There's quite a lot of turnover; it's hard work and some people just aren't cut out for it. They should be at drinks tonight; I told Tom I'd see him there.'

'Excellent.' Sadie wiggles her eyebrows at Lauren.

'Are you single, then?'

'Yep. Recently. I'd been going out with a guy for five years, but it was a total farce by the end. We never even lived together, and neither of us could be bothered to really make time for the other. He's a trader in the City, and I tend to put in long hours at work, so we didn't have much quality time together. I think we liked the idea of it more than the reality. So I'm ready to have some fun and put myself first.'

'Quite right.' Lauren holds the door to the Oast House open. 'You've picked a great time to join the team. Zoe and Jess are amazing, but they were always so stressed until we got Evelyn's investment. And Evelyn's beautiful, isn't she? It's so much more glamorous since she came on the scene. I just love her style. Her shoe collection is to die for.'

The team drinks are being held in a reserved space at one end of the room, by the enormous fireplace. It must be heavenly to curl up on one of these enormous sofas in winter, in front of a roaring log fire. There's no fire today, and the endless double doors are open given the warmth of the weather. The early arrivals stand in clusters and there's an abundant spread of nibbles, wine and beer on the coffee table by the fire.

Sadie clocks Danny immediately. He's standing with Angus, who has his arm around Evelyn, and a few others. His dirty blonde hair looks damp, and he's changed out of his Sorrel Farm gear into cargo shorts and a pristine white t-shirt that clings to his toned body. He shoots her a grin that seemed full of intention, though she can't articulate in what way. She smiles back before averting her gaze to the drinks.

'Wine?' she asks Lauren.

'Totes, thanks,' Lauren replies. 'There's Tom—I'll introduce you.'

Drinks poured, she follows Lauren over to the group. A wiry bloke with ginger hair and a ruddy face kisses Lauren.

After Lauren introduces them, Tom says, 'So, Sadie—how was your first day? You survive?'

Sadie shoots a glance at Evelyn. 'It went well, I think. There's a lot to learn. I worked for the press before this, so it's odd for me to be on this side.'

Tom jerks his thumb at Danny. 'My new boss started today, too. This is Danny.'

'Oh, we've already met.' Danny grins at her. She attempts not to react, besides a small nod of acknowledgement.

He steps forward and raised his bottle of beer. 'To new beginnings,' he says, holding her gaze.

She clinks her wineglass against the bottle. 'Indeed,' she says stiffly. It won't do to flirt in front of Evelyn—even if she has her head leaning on Angus' shoulder—and she's damned if she'll make it as easy for Danny as other females probably do.

He stays where he is, in her body space, blocking Tom.

'So,' he says. 'Tell me what you're doing here, and what you did for the press.'

'I was a journalist.' Her mouth has gone dry; she takes a sip of wine. 'For the *Tribune*—that's how I met Evelyn. I did a feature on her. Now I'm running PR for the farm. The theory is, my experience will help me get inside the journalists' heads and pitch them exactly the kind of pieces that they want; I'll be able to spoon-feed them and they'll like working with me.'

'And the practice?'

She smiles wryly. 'The reality is that I have no press contacts beyond the *Tribune*. But there's great momentum behind the brand with Evelyn's arrival, so hopefully I can surf that and not disgrace myself.'

He seems to be listening avidly, watching with those

blue eyes and nodding as she speaks. It's all quite intense. He folds his arms across his chest and her eyes flick to his pecs and biceps, both apparent through the fabric of his t-shirt. Either manual labour really works for him, or he works out. And he's very brown; no tan lines are visible around his sleeves or neck. She's possibly answered her own earlier question about his builder's tan. Her cheeks grow warm and she hurriedly returns her gaze to his face.

'I don't know you,' he says, 'but something tells me you won't disgrace yourself. You look like you get whatever you want.'

'I try,' she says. 'I'm very determined.'

'I like a woman who knows exactly what she wants.' He slowly raises his beer bottle to his lips without breaking eye contact. He's so close she can smell shower gel and fresh laundry rising off his body. She has an overwhelming urge to rest her hand on the expanse of skin where his neck meets his shoulder, and slip her fingers under the collar of his t-shirt.

'Tell me about yourself,' she says hastily. She won't rise to his comment. Something tells her he's already aware of the effect he's having on her, without her handing herself to him on a platter.

He raises his eyebrows at her as if to say: *your diversionary tactics don't fool me.*

'Not much to tell. My whole career has been in agriculture since I left Cirencester. I was managing a local organic farm, but I saw the press in the summer around Sorrel Farm and what Angus and Zoe were trying to achieve. I'm fascinated by biodynamics. So when I heard through the old Cirencester network that Angus was hiring, I jumped at the chance—it's an amazing opportunity to learn from him and see the effects of his efforts in real time.'

'What's the difference between your job and his?'

'His role was too big. I'm taking over some of it—the more day-to-day management. It frees Angus up to focus on the more strategic stuff. Biodynamics are a slow business. They say it takes seven years to see the ecosystem of a biodynamic farm working as it should. Angus and Zoe are about two years in. The theory is that having me on board means he can plant the most important seeds—pun intended—in good time.'

'And the practice?' she asks archly, and he laughs.

'Fuck knows. I strongly suspect Angus hired me primarily to liberate him from the bonds of pre-dawn starts—or, at least, Evelyn made him outsource that part of the role.'

'Ugh.' She makes a face. 'I don't envy you. You'll have to be a very good boy—hot cup of cocoa, and bed at nine.'

His eyes bore into her. 'I can think of far more enjoyable ways to wind down in bed than a fucking cup of cocoa. Want to know what they are?'

She squirms, unable to tear her gaze away. Once again, she has the sensation that he knows exactly the effect he's having on her with his innuendo, and his proximity, and that outrageous tan.

She's saved by Tom slapping a pale, freckled hand on Danny's shoulder.

'Come and have a smoke outside, mate. And leave Sadie alone.'

Danny winks at her. 'Later,' he says, and is gone.

Lauren sidles over with a bottle of wine and proceeds to top Sadie up.

'Just a bit,' Sadie says. 'I'm driving.'

'Getting cosy with Danny, were we?' Lauren asks.

Sadie sighs. 'Trying not to. Something tells me he's bad

news. He is bloody gorgeous, though, and he's an outrageous flirt.'

'Nothing wrong with some harmless flirting. Just be careful. Tom said he mentioned a girlfriend in passing today.'

She's surprised by the pang of disappointment that hits her in the gut. 'Wow,' she manages. 'Poor girlfriend. He flirts like he's available.'

'I don't know more,' Lauren says. 'I can ask Tom to find out if you like? I'll tell him to be discreet.'

'Sure.' Sadie feigns nonchalance. She certainly doesn't want to get involved with anyone after the monotony of her relationship with David, and she doesn't want to threaten her professional reputation by messing around at work, but there's a wide enough gulf between the farm team and the marketing side, surely? Danny would be the perfect guy to rebound with—smoking hot and unlikely to want anything serious. She missed this while she was with David: the adrenalin rush of flirting; the thrill of not knowing whether she's hit her target.

'Leave it with me. You know who else I think is adorable?' Lauren continues. 'Ned.'

'Who the fuck is Ned?'

'Ned! You know, our Finance Director—I saw Evelyn introduce you to him earlier.'

'Oh, yeah.' A vague recollection of meeting someone on the finance side surfaces. 'No thanks. He's all yours.'

'He's cute,' Lauren insists. 'And he's behind me. I've seen him looking over—you're a popular girl.' She jerks her head backwards.

Sadie looks over Lauren's shoulder. Christ, no. He's a tall guy in a boxy shirt that has press-marks down the front. His collar is button-down and a white t-shirt peeks out from under it. If he was any more square, he'd have corners. He's a walking geek.

'He's awful,' Sadie says. 'He looks completely humourless.' She likes intelligence, but she's more a fan of the commercial kind; David's brand of intelligence was street-smart and flashy. The City was the perfect home for him. Geekiness for the sake of geekiness is simply unattractive. The guy—Ned—catches her eye and looks down at his glass of red wine without smiling. He's standing with Angus and Evelyn.

'He's really nice—super kind and patient,' Lauren says. 'And he's an amazing swimmer. Sometimes I go and sit by the indoor pool after work with a glass of wine and watch him do laps. It's hot.'

Sadie laughs so hard she almost spits out her wine. 'What does Tom have to say about that?'

'It's my guilty pleasure.' Lauren smiles dreamily. 'He doesn't have to know. I'll take you one evening. We can have a drink and perv over Ned in his speedos. Have you been into the spa yet? It's lush—the pool is in an orangery.'

'No. And I have no interest in perving over Ned, as you put it. Speedos—ugh.' What a revolting mental image.

'You'll see.' Lauren nods sagely.

NED IS DOING his best to engage in conversation with Angus and Evelyn, who are both on fine form, but his attention is on the new PR manager, Sadie. She and Lauren beat him to the Oast House by a few minutes; he saw them leave the office and by the time he made it to drinks, she was all over Angus' new assistant. Danny Scott, his name is.

He stands by his earlier impression that she's made of

pure gold. She's back-lit in the late afternoon sunshine that pours through the huge glass doors, and it looks as if a halo hovers around her blonde head. He takes in her tanned, shapely limbs in that little dress; fine gold bands glinted on the slim wrist holding the wineglass. Her arms and legs are back-lit too; he's too far away to see the actual hairs on her arms, but the sunshine illuminates them as a soft blur. She's incandescent.

As he gazes at her, he tries to analyse what particular alchemy it is that's hooked his attention so instantly. It's a combination, he decides, of the regularity of her features, her innate poise, and some spirit of absolute self-sufficiency that he senses rather than knows. Shame it comes at the price of utter charmlessness. Her indifference earlier bordered on rudeness.

She isn't being charmless now. She still has the stand-offish look on her face, but her body is betraying her. She's leaning into Danny, and he keeps coming closer. Suddenly, her face breaks out in a smile and she's radiant: dimples, the like of which he's never seen. They utterly transform her face. He's not stupid. He can tell the guy is obnoxiously good-looking, but does he have to make a beeline for the first woman Ned's found attractive in months and months—ever since he finished with Natalie, in fact? He tells himself it doesn't make any difference; she couldn't be less interested in him, so it doesn't matter who she *is* interested in. In any case, he'll have to see her every day at work, so it's best to keep things strictly professional.

Evelyn interrupts his musings with a hand on his arm, her scent wafting his way. She always smells wonderful—expensive and floral.

'We were just saying how intense these last few weeks have been for you. Honestly, you've been an absolute star. I couldn't have done this transition without you. Did you get any summer holiday at all? I don't want us to break you!'

He smiles at her. 'It's been my pleasure, and it's very exciting to see the funds pouring in after Angus, Jess and Zoe have worked so hard to get us to this point. You're like our fairy godmother, flying in to make all our problems go away.'

Angus tightens his grip around Evelyn's shoulder and smiles down at her. 'You're certainly my fairy godmother.'

Ned feels a pang of envy. Lucky Angus, to be so profoundly in love, although he certainly deserves it. When Ned arrived at the farm, Angus was adjusting to his new life after his wife had walked out on him. It hit him hard: he confided to Ned over beers how difficult he was finding it to recalibrate to a reality of being alone in his forties, having spent the past two decades building a family with Audrey. Ned is delighted he's finding happiness with Evelyn. Their relationship is young, but it strikes him that Angus and Evelyn seem already to have a true partnership. They're good for each other.

'Penny for them.' Evelyn nudges him gently.

'What?' His gaze has drifted over to Sadie again; he drags it reluctantly back to Evelyn.

'She's stunning, isn't she?' There's a little smile on her lips.

'Who?' he asks, warmth creeping up his neck.

She raises her eyebrows at him as if to say, *oh, come on.* 'Sadie.'

'I suppose so,' he concedes. 'She seems prickly, though.'

Evelyn laughs. 'She's a punchy one—she doesn't suffer fools. Not that anyone could ever class you as a fool. But she's a softie, under the surface. I'm sure you'll thaw her out, eventually.'

'I wouldn't hold your breath,' he mutters. 'But it looks like Danny's having a good shot at melting her *froideur*.'

'I'll have to keep an eye on him,' Angus says. 'Maybe I should have put a morality clause in his contract.'

Ned gives a dry chuckle and nods in Evelyn's direction. 'Pot and kettle, mate.'

'Nothing immoral about true love,' Angus says.

'Well, we can't all be as sickeningly happy as you two,' Ned says affectionately.

'Do you have anyone on the scene, Ned?' Evelyn asks.

'Not at present. I was with someone for a couple of years—Natalie—but we broke up a few months ago. She wanted us to get married, and I knew I couldn't give her that, so I felt it was best to break it off.'

Evelyn rolls her eyes. 'Men,' she says good-naturedly. 'It's always the same story.'

'It wasn't my fault,' he protests. 'Marriage and kids—I want all that; I'm thirty-four, for Christ's sake. I'm ready to commit to someone. But she wasn't the one.'

Evelyn pats him on the arm. 'You're a catch. Any woman would be lucky to have you—you're so loyal and kind, and obscenely intelligent, and I'd tell you how attractive you are if Angus wasn't standing next to me.'

'Oi!' Angus says.

'It'll happen for you,' she says. 'Just have faith, my dear.'

6

Evelyn rests her head on Angus' shoulder and listens as Jess regales them with an expletive-laden account of her day dealing with the maintenance contract for the resort's two pools. She and Zoe couldn't be more different. Zoe towers above most females. Jess is five foot two—a little pocket rocket. Zoe is all willowy limbs, and Jess is all curves. Zoe's dark; Jess is fair. Zoe's preferred state is serene silence; Jess is a relentless extrovert.

And yet, when Jess brought Zoe home from her travels nearly twenty years ago, Evelyn saw a change in her friend that left her in no doubt that this beautiful, mysterious woman grounded and completed Jess in a way she couldn't have foreseen. If Jess exudes the full force of the sun, then Zoe is a creature of the moon, and she seems to share some of the moon's invisible but undeniable powers. She's a white witch: eternally benevolent, and in tune with the healing powers of nature to an extent that makes Evelyn shiver if she thinks about it too much.

She attempts to tune Jess out and home in on Zoe, so still, but so magnetic. There's so much under the surface there, and if Zoe would only let her—and the public—in, they'd be sitting on a treasure trove; she's sure of it. Zoe's an intoxicating cocktail of beauty and enigma and talent and goodness, and by God, could Evelyn spin that into a marketing dream. And yet Zoe remains a closed door in so many ways, even after almost two decades of friendship.

Evelyn's aware that Zoe wasn't happy with the way she answered for her in the meeting with Avery earlier this week; she pushed Zoe into a corner by agreeing in so many words that Zoe should front the book. She knows it was bad form and an abuse of her friendship; she should have been acting as Zoe's advocate in that meeting; not prostituting her friend and colleague for a book deal. She's not proud of essentially offering Avery whatever she wants, but this is why Jess and Zoe have brought her on board: to build the brand and the business. They're sitting on a goldmine with Zoe and it's Evelyn's job to realise that value. She'll just have to make Zoe come around to it.

Zoe's not angry—she's never seen Zoe get angry about anything in all the years she's known her—but she's politely inscrutable, and the sting of her disappointment has been palpable, the last couple of days. It's not a pleasant feeling, letting Zoe down. She has to make amends while continuing to fight the fight to get Sorrel Farm on the map.

They sit around the wooden table in the stunning glass box Jess and Zoe have added to the back of Jess' parents' original farm house. In summer, it's the perfect vantage point to admire the view of the old gardens that run down to the ancient ha-ha, and the fields beyond. When they got here earlier this evening, they enjoyed the fruit and walnut trees dotted around the lawns, bursting with ripened produce. But now it's dark, and the walls reflect the beloved shapes of her friends by candlelight. Their plates are scraped clean of Zoe's delicious food, and she luxuriates in the heavenly sensation of Angus' arm around her as he sips his glass of red. She feels full, and safe, and loved. He kisses her temple, and she snuggles further into him.

Zoe is gazing lovingly at Jess as she holds the floor. Her attitude to her wife tends to be one of fond, amused tolerance of Jess' overreactions to life. Jess takes a gulp of wine.

'My chat stinks. For fuck's sake, why don't none of you tell me to shut up? What's the latest with the cookbook, Evie?'

Her tone sounds innocuous enough. If Zoe's been complaining to her, they'd know about it. Jess doesn't hold back, especially when defending her wife. Evelyn gives Zoe a smile to say, *I'm not about to throw you under the bus.* She reaches down and pulls an envelope out of her bag.

'Well, on that note, I have something I want to show you guys.'

She pulls a large piece of paper out of the envelope and turns it over, pushing it across the table towards Jess and Zoe. It's a photograph, a new shot Clara took of Zoe in the walled garden a couple of weeks ago. It's the first time Zoe's seen it. She's squatting next to a planting bed in a t-shirt and jeans and her apron, balancing a shallow basket of leeks on her knees. A trowel nestles in one hand. It was taken before she had her braids done, and her tight curls look enormous, back-lit golden against the late summer sun. The beds behind her, out of focus, are a blur of green.

Jess inhales sharply. 'You're so beautiful, darling. That's exquisite.'

'It's stunning, Zoe,' Angus says with feeling.

Evelyn smiles. 'I totally agree. I'm not saying this is a cover shot, but *you* are definitely a cover girl, Zoe Augustin.

You're magic. I know you don't want to hear this, but we can't do this book unless you're the face of it, inside and out.'

Zoe visibly retreats. She lays her hands, palms down, on the smooth wood of the table, something Evelyn noticed she did during the meeting the other day too.

'I don't want to be the face,' she says quietly. 'I don't want this book to be about me. I can be a mouthpiece for this philosophy for living and eating that we all believe in so strongly; nothing more. It's not about me.'

'If this isn't something Zoe wants, then it doesn't happen.' Jess is the fierce tigress tonight. 'End of story. We find another way around it, or we ditch the book idea altogether.'

It's incredibly frustrating. Zoe and Jess work so hard, but it's this lack of commerciality that's kept the farm and resort from meeting its potential up until now. She needs to tread gently, to avoid making Zoe run for the hills.

'Is it mainly about the cover?' she asks. 'Maybe we can rethink using a close-up of you; maybe it can be a more distant shot of you on the land. But I really, really would caution against that, Zoe. You are the force that pulls the farm and resort together—you make the case for eating off the land more compellingly than anyone could. Yes, there are chefs out there who don't put their face on the cover of their books, but Sorrel Farm hasn't built up the necessary profile as a destination yet to carry the book on its own. I know you'll hate this phrase, but it requires a cult of personality to drive this, and that personality is you.

'You'll give it soul and make it more aspirational than we could ever make it if it's just shots of produce and plates. You'll elevate it beyond the zillions of cook books out there, and you'll capture the reader's imagination. Then the devotees of the farm will come flocking. That's what we need. Think of the book as a business card for the farm.'

Angus releases her and tops up the wineglasses. 'What's wrong with an abstract cover? That's what Ottolenghi does.'

'Ottolenghi has made a name for himself already.' Evelyn is growing more frustrated. 'And it's not just the book, guys; it's the press. We need to court the press very hard while the book's in the works, to build up our process. I'm afraid Zoe is the person best-placed to do that. Sadie and I can do the heavy-lifting, but our business is all about food, and Zoe needs to get comfortable fronting the brand. Otherwise we're just a nice little resort and a business-to-business food producer.'

'Is that so bad?' Jess asks.

'Oh, come on. That's not why you gave me thirty percent of your company. And to be honest, it's not why I came on board. And it's definitely not what I paid for—that valuation you came up with has a lot of future growth baked into it. I want to do great things for you guys, but you need to want to help yourselves. Zoe, I swear, I will be by your side through every step of this; you'll have full input, but if you want the amazing work that you three are doing to have a platform, then I'm afraid having a founder-led brand strategy is the quickest and most effective way to achieve that. It will make the brand aspirational but accessible, and it'll give people a sense of human connection—no one does that better than you. Seriously, I know what I'm doing here. I did it for Seb, and I can do it for you. I just need you to take this leap of faith with me.'

Zoe sighs and smooths her braids over one shoulder. This is the nearest she gets to being ruffled. 'And the text? Who writes the text? Whose voice is it?'

'We use a ghost-writer,' Evelyn tells her. 'But it needs to

be your voice. In my head, the first section is a wander through the farm and its produce—both livestock and crops. It sets the scene and explains the importance of provenance, of communion. The recipes stem from that. And that has to be your voice, really. We can include sections from Angus, to talk us through the importance of biodiversity and of cultivating the healthiest soil for our produce, and it'd be wonderful to have Jess explaining the farm's history and the decision to shift to organic and then biodynamics. But this can't be some generic romp through the farm. It has to have a voice; it has to feel *personal*. And no one can do that better than you. If this is a magical parcel of land where incredible things are happening, then you're the *chatelaine* of all that.'

'I'm not sure.' Zoe presses her fingers to her temples. 'I'm sorry Evie; I'm just not sure. It's hurting my head. Let me sleep on it, ok? I'm going to go wash up now.'

She gets to her feet and heads into the kitchen, a pile of platters in her hand.

Jess glares at Evelyn. 'Nice one.'

Evelyn is stunned. She holds her hands up. 'I'm sorry. But I have no idea why she's so upset. Maybe I should go and talk to her.'

'No.' Angus puts his hand on her arm. 'Just leave her, sweetheart.'

A look passes between Jess and Angus. She's facing Jess, and it looks like a private acknowledgement, an understanding. A moment from which Evelyn is definitely excluded.

~

As they get in the car, she tries to make sense of what the hell just happened.

'Tell me what I'm missing.' She puts the gearstick aggressively into Drive mode. 'I know Zoe doesn't love the spotlight, but it felt like there was a damn sight more going on in that conversation than I was privy to.'

Angus puts a comforting arm on her thigh. 'It's a big ask, sweetheart. You've spent years watching Seb navigate that world; you're used to it. And Seb's a very different character from Zoe. Tell me I'm wrong, but the guy loves being the centre of attention. She's an extremely private, low-key person.'

She sighs. 'You're not wrong there. But Seb has explicitly cultivated a sense of celebrity. We're not talking that level of fame for Zoe, but she is exceptionally talented, and she has star quality. You can't deny that. This isn't me trying to foist stardom on someone; it's the natural next step for someone of her talents, with this incredible ready-made brand around them. I had to create all that for Seb—that whole lifestyle thing. Zoe has it right here on the farm. It's a marketer's dream.'

'I know you're right,' he says.

'So? Why didn't you and Jess put a foot in my corner? I'm not trying to bully her; this is for everyone's good. I thought you guys were on board with the book idea.'

'We are. We're just—we're both very protective of Zoe.'

Angus and Zoe go back a long way, having read Theology together at Oxford, before Zoe returned to her native Provence and discovered that recipe books fed her soul far more than ancient religious texts.

'Of course you are. And so am I. But you're both acting a little odd. What was with that look you gave each other?'

'What look?'

'Just before we left. I don't know—it was like you both had the same reason for digging your heels in.'

Angus is silent for a moment. His hand pats her thigh in a comforting manner. 'Look, sweetheart. It's entirely acceptable for Zoe have her reasons for not wanting to do this, and for her to want to keep those reasons private. And we don't have to know what they are to respect her decision.'

She glances at him. He's staring straight ahead; headlights of an oncoming car illuminate his profile.

'Ok, so now you've got me curious. Are you telling me you know why Zoe's being so reticent about all this?'

'I have an idea, yes.'

'What's the reason, then?'

'It's not my place to say.'

'*Seriously*?'

'Sweetheart.' He puts a warm hand around the back of her neck and she shivers despite herself. 'When it comes to my own secrets, well, I have none from you. You can ask me anything. But I'm not about to betray my friends' confidences, no matter how much I love you. I'm telling you, just let it rest a while. This is Zoe's decision to make, and she'll come around, or not, in her own good time.'

He's right, of course. It would be unfair of her to pressure him into betraying Zoe's confidence, and she doesn't want to pick a fight with him. But now her curiosity is well and truly piqued: she can smell a story, and she won't rest until she gets to the bottom of it.

7

After a fortnight of being in her new seat full-time, Evelyn still feels like a racehorse in the starting box. She's so full of adrenalin and ideas and ambitions that she doesn't know where to start or how to catch a breath—and she absolutely loves it. There's nothing like a new challenge to light a fire under her, and here she is, in this beautiful resort, surrounded by her oldest friends and the love of her life, with more opportunities glinting at her than she could count. Her cup is running over.

Thank goodness for Angus, who's proving the yin to her yang. Even Jess, who's the biggest fan of her and Angus' relationship, urged her to take it slowly.

'You've been through so much, Evie,' she said. 'Your and Eddie's lives were turned upside down this summer, and thank fuck it's all worked out for the best, but you're hitting a fuck-load of fresh starts all at once. You need to pace yourself, for Eddie's sake and for the sake of your relationship.'

Behind her trademark, and usually gratuitous, swearing, Jess has a heart the size of the ocean and knows Evelyn better than anyone on earth, so she tries to heed her advice.

However, it seems not to be necessary. She and Angus have fallen into a rhythm so smooth, she could swear they've been together for years. She can't believe how compatible they are. She wants to work hard on their relationship, but it feels as though she doesn't have to.

Of course, some of the bliss stems from the fact that they're still very much in their honeymoon period. They're still drunk on each other; they can't believe their luck. That they get to share their work life as well as their personal life makes her cup overflow even more. But more than that, they feel like a team. He has her back, and she has his. He's her staunchest ally and biggest cheerleader. He isn't fazed by her wealth or by the scale of her ambition: she understands that the latter is one of the things he's fallen for in her.

Still, his priority is her wellbeing and she can feel him gently attempt to rein her in when she risks exploding with the excitement and pressure of all the goals she's setting herself. Their perspectives are very different on that front. When she and Seb were running Seb Macleod Limited, they were always at the mercy of their major investor. Private equity companies are known for relentless focus on growth and profitability, and continuously delivering for them felt like being on a hamster wheel. Angus, meanwhile, plays a long game. As a farmer, he has to.

'Relax!' he'll whisper to her as he holds her to him. 'Sorrel Farm doesn't have to be a global name by Christmas. We have time. You've already made great strides. Just remember not to be so focused on making crazy promises to Jess, and pushing Zoe, that you forget to enjoy the ride.'

He's right, of course. It's mildly irritating how frequently he's right. She's met so many CEOs and founders of enormous companies over the years, and they all say the same thing: the early, scrappy days were the best, before their corporate babies became automated juggernauts. It's so easy to get swept away by what Sorrel Farm could become, but right now they're in the sweet spot—the magical zone of having full autonomy plus a healthy cash balance to fund their dreams.

One thing she's underestimated is how much being physically immersed in Sorrel Farm affects her for the better. The resort's charm and the restorative nature of the farmland seep into her veins and bring her blood pressure down far more easily than any amount of yoga did in London. In addition, setting up home with Angus and Eddie, amidst beautiful grounds far superior to her former back garden in Holland Park, is proving a profoundly joyful process. While Angus thinks the house is lovely, it needs work to bring it up to her standards. Even so, it's a beautiful base and the warm September weather has allowed them to spend several evenings outside since moving in, closing off the day on the west-facing terrace with a chilled glass of wine, in exactly the way she saw in her mind's eye when the property first came on her radar.

Eddie has taken to running manically around the grounds after school and making good use of the old sunken trampoline the previous owners left. Seeing the ease with which Angus and Eddie get along is also an enormous source of relief and joy to her. Eddie has been through so much this summer, and her heart bursts to see the endless patience and generosity with which Angus plays with him and educates him on the gardens. Watching them potter about the grounds together like two old men, poking around in the planting beds, is a wonder. Eddie worships Angus and regards him as the absolute authority on all things nature-related. And, from what Angus tells her, the appreciation is mutual. His boys, Hector and Alistair, are in their third and second years of university respectively and she knows Angus sees Eddie as a second chance at parenting. In short, life is more full of love and joy and anticipation at what lies ahead than she could ever have hoped for.

One balmy day in mid-September, she sits down for lunch with Sadie in Sorrel Farm's walled garden. It's mild enough to wear her little cardigan draped over her shoulders. The umbrellas are still up and diners populate the tables dotted around the beautiful garden, its pool sparkling aqua and its ancient walls glowing in the hazy late-summer sunshine.

She munches on a plump olive and tops up their glasses with sparkling water. When she first came down to the farm to escape the press frenzy over the news that Seb was gay, she gorged on gluten and rosé at every opportunity. These days, she tries to stick to a healthier, more energising diet. At the same time, she's more relaxed and kinder to herself than she was in London. She enjoys regular treats—it's impossible to ignore the croissants and granola and puddings completely in this place—and she doesn't beat herself up over them. It's a more balanced approach than she allowed herself to have in London; after all, she and Seb built their brand on healthy eating.

'How are you settling in?' she asks Sadie.

'Good, I think.' Sadie adjusts the gold bangles on her wrist. Today she's in a sleek black boiler-suit with vertiginous heels that look amazing but are ill-suited to the cobbles in the courtyard. *Mini-me*, Evelyn thinks fondly. The black is the perfect foil for the immaculate, pale golden bob that she has, as usual, scraped back into a short ponytail.

'Are you getting to know the team—are people looking after you?' Evelyn asks.

Sadie shrugs. 'Everyone's fine. More than fine. But I

haven't come here to make friends. I'll build the relationships I need to build and invest the time so I can market this place to the best of my ability. But my focus the last couple of weeks has been getting to know the press, rather than my colleagues.'

Evelyn smiles. Sadie is a machine. She'll be highly effective at this role; she just needs to make sure she invests the necessary time in building human relationships. Sadie seems to be of the opinion that relationships are a waste of time; in reality, they're everything.

'Getting to know your colleagues will make your life here far happier,' she says now. 'I feel responsible for you; I'm the one who dragged you down here. How are you getting on with your new flatmates?'

Sadie grimaces. 'Ok, I suppose. I hardly see them. They both work in Canary Wharf. It's a bit awkward, living with a couple. It's obvious they only rented the room out to get some extra cash. But they leave me alone, and I've spent the last two weekends in London, staying with girlfriends. I'll look for somewhere else to live once I've had time to get settled in the job.'

It sounds a bit grim. 'You must come over for supper one evening,' Evelyn tells her. 'Come and see the new house before the evenings draw in too much.'

'I'd love to,' Sadie says, 'as long as you let me loose in your dressing room. You must need an entire wing for all your clothes. I mean, look at that Chanel cardigan. It's divine.'

Lunch arrives: the *plat du jour* is lightly grilled Dover sole with roasted squash and braised leeks from the walled garden. They both lean back as the server puts down their plates.

'I'll tell you what,' Evelyn says. 'I'll let you loose in my dressing room when you get me what I want.'

Sadie leans forward. 'Tell me what you want and I'll get it for you.'

Evelyn picks up her fork and spears a piece of meltingly light fish. 'The *Sunday Times Magazine*. Zoe on the cover in the next six months.'

She hears a sharp intake of breath from Sadie as she reflects on the taste sensation that is her Dover sole.

'She didn't look too happy in the meeting with Penguin a couple of weeks ago,' Sadie says. 'What was going on there?'

'She's shy and modest. She doesn't see her own appeal, and she hates any kind of attention. The idea of having her face on the cover of a book—or a magazine—is her worst nightmare.' The truth is, she's no closer to understanding the reasons behind Zoe's reticence. She's respected Angus and Jess' pleas to back off, and she hasn't pushed it. Zoe has been her usual, charming self and, against every commercial instinct she has, Evelyn has desisted from pushing her. Her current theory is that she scared Zoe off by proposing they launch Zoe's career in the public eye with a fully fledged book. They can continue to work away on the book in the background, especially to build their photographic content, but she hopes that securing a feature in a broadsheet supplement will be a more palatable prospect for Zoe to swallow.

~

As they eat, they discuss the upcoming highlights in the farm's marketing calendar. Sadie feels more invigorated than she has in days. She loves spending time with Evelyn—her style and energy make her a bridge back to London.

Sadie's missing the city far more than she expected. The farm is beautiful, but it doesn't seem like the real world, and she feels no rapport with Sevenoaks at all. But Evelyn is why she's here, and if this opportunity is sufficient to hold Evelyn's attention, it's good enough for Sadie to have a decent shot at.

They discuss the next major event, which is the Harvest Festival, the first Saturday in October. It's first and foremost a community event; local primary schools have received some free tickets, and it's a chance to engage local families and children with the workings of the farm. There will also be food and drink stalls in the walled garden to showcase the farm's latest produce and celebrate the harvest. They've invited local and foodie national press. It's a lovely opportunity for the press to experience the synergies between the farm and resort. Their room occupancy is far higher these days than it was at the start of the summer, but they've held back a selection of rooms for the more important journalists attending. Sadie has been chasing the journalists Evelyn approached earlier in the season, and she's pleased with the press list as it stands.

'We should get Angus another interview with Penny from *Food* magazine while she's here,' Evelyn says. 'She adores him. They can talk about manure to their hearts' content.'

'You two are sweet together. Random, but sweet. Chanel and manure.'

Evelyn looks at her, and Sadie sees mischief twinkling in her eyes.

'My random but sweet boyfriend tells me Danny's been following you around and asking him for intel on you. Sadie had a little lamb...'

'Oh, God.' Sadie colours. 'Subtle that guy is not.'

Evelyn leans back and surveys her. 'Do tell. I have to live vicariously through you now.'

He is following her around, as much as it's possible for a member of the farming team to do. She's already learnt that they hang out *en masse*—they're a combination of agricultural graduates, migrant workers, professional farmers, gardeners, and interns. They're Angus' flock, all bearing a coffee-and-white uniform which seems highly impractical for those toiling in the fields and presumably will be exchanged for something more durable as the weather got colder.

Not that she's complaining. The snug white polo shirt and cargo shorts look as though they've been made for Danny. She's seen his shirt pristine at the start of the day and earth streaked at the end: she's not sure which is sexier. He certainly pops into the office far more than any of his colleagues have reason to do: to check the roster, pass information to Ned, or grab a chat with Jess. To be fair, he is on the management side of things so there's presumably a lot more paperwork for him than for the rest of the team.

But every time he comes in, he makes a beeline for wherever Sadie's sitting that day. He leans on the glossy white table, so close that she's become intimately familiar with his scent: soil, sweat, soap. Clean and dirty. She's like a bloodhound; she can pick up on it almost as soon as he enters the office. He settles that arse on the table and she scoots back in her chair, both so they can make eye contact and to put a few more inches between them, to protect her from the heat that rises off his body.

Thank God his shorts come to just below the knee, but his tanned, hairy calves give her some idea of what his thighs would be like. And when her eyes travel upwards, they encounter equally tanned forearms folded over a flat stomach before the fabric swells and strains over his pecs. She knows what she'll find when her eyes reach his face: a smile that, a century ago, would have had her swooning and reaching for her smelling salts, and summer-blue eyes, crinkling with amusement at the reaction he's having on her.

He hasn't tried anything yet, technically. Innuendo, yes. Compliments. Banter. Teasing. And the odd brag thrown in for good measure. But he hasn't propositioned her or asked her out. Her mole network has gone quiet on whether he has a girlfriend and she hasn't summoned up the courage to ask him herself. Asking him if he's single is flagrantly admitting interest. And so she plays along, toying with him, batting back his comments, giving him one message with her words and another with her eyes and body.

It's childish, it's probably unprofessional, and the less base part of her tells her it's a bad idea. But it's also *hot*, far hotter than the past year or two were with David. And so she continues to play the game.

'He's trouble,' she tells Evelyn now. 'I'm steering well clear.' And she doesn't mean a word of it.

The conversation moves around to work, and to the editorial pipeline.

'I had an email from the FT.' Evelyn picks up her phone. 'Let me forward it to you. They have a column called *FT on FDs* and they've told me they'll feature Ned. The column has been very FTSE 100-heavy and they're trying to include a wider variety of businesses. Can I leave it with you?'

Ugh. A column on Ned's day job sounds turgid beyond belief, but any way of getting access to the *Financial Times* is a big deal. She shrugs. 'Sure. Leave it with me.' She'll get it done, but her neurons are firing over an altogether more tantalising project: how the hell to get Zoe onto the cover of the *Sunday Times Magazine.*

8

In the weeks after Sadie's arrival, Ned fails to make any headway with his feelings. It's ridiculous: she's a total stranger who hasn't said more than a handful of words directly to him, and she appears utterly lacking in the basics of manners and decency. She's the opposite of his usual type: warm and vivacious women who are a mother's dream. Sadie is punchy as hell and, as Evelyn warned him, does not suffer fools. He's seen her be brusque with several of their colleagues. The only people she has any time for are Evelyn, Lauren, with whom she's forged an unlikely friendship, and that slick fucker Danny, who's been hanging around her like a bad smell. They're the only ones who can light her up and bring out those gorgeous dimples.

And yet, the intensity of his feelings for her increases with each passing day, or so it feels. He's not used to this. His days in the office have always flown by in a haze of productivity and professional fulfilment. He loves everything about his job: the therapy of immersing himself in numbers as much as the people with whom he works. And he believes in Sorrel Farm like nothing else. Over the past few weeks, however, his flow state has eluded him; he's been antsy and distracted. A horrifying proportion of his brain function seems given over to obsessing over Sadie: where she's sitting, what she's doing, how she looks. No amount of stern self-talk or application of logic can dial it down. Decades of pre-dawn swim-meets have built his discipline muscles and these days he's a machine, capable of directing his full attention wherever it's needed. But his new addiction is erasing these hard-won habits. She's got under his skin, and he cannot bloody well shift her.

When he and Evelyn signed off on the hire of a new PR manager and put her salary in the budget, Evelyn told him she was hiring the same journalist who had done the wonderful *Tribune* cover feature on her, the feature that got them all so excited and marked a huge upswing in reservations at the resort. He pulls the article up on the *Tribune*'s website and reads it again with fresh eyes. Evelyn told him she was impressed by Sadie's directness (it's hard to argue with that description) and hungry commerciality. The feature is fantastic: it's concise and compelling, but there's a softness to her writing that's unexpected. She sees the magic in Evelyn and in the farm, and she conveys it beautifully. Essentially, she knows exactly how to sell the Sorrel Farm dream. No wonder Evelyn wants her on the other side, conjuring up the same must-have magic for press all over the world.

He falls down a Sadie-shaped rabbit hole, searching for her by-line. There's an excellent interview with Victoria Beckham from earlier in the year, and many more lifestyle pieces and entrepreneurial features. The Beckham interview once again captures the essence of the woman she's interviewing. Reading her writing feels almost voyeuristic. At work she's a closed book, giving almost nothing of herself to her colleagues, but her writing tells another story. It suggests that beneath that icy exterior lies a warm, passionate heart and a well-hidden gift for communicating.

On Mondays, the senior staff members gather for a late working lunch on the mezzanine of the Oast House. It's a chance to update each other on progress in their various areas and to share opportunities for synergies. Ned uses it as an opportunity to share where revenue is tracking against their targets, and to update the budget with any projects or requests that come up in the meeting. Jess, Zoe, Angus, Danny, Evelyn, Sadie and attend, as well as the line managers for hospitality, procurement and resort operations.

The meeting itself is uneventful. Angus requests a budget increase to cover some additional machinery, which Ned signs off on. The sales of fresh produce are exceeding their forecasts, thanks to the extra profile that having Seb Macleod Ltd as a client has brought them, so there's slack in the budget to cover extra investment on the farming side. Angus is more fired up about the outlook than Ned can remember seeing—he suspects Angus is benefiting from the novelty of extra sleep and headspace that having Danny on board affords him, as well as the clear devotion of a good, and very beautiful, woman. Lucky bastard.

Sadie's circumspect for the most part. She still seems to be taking a lot in. When it's her turn, she updates the team on their highest PR priorities for the fourth quarter. Their biggest focus is securing a high-profile food feature on Zoe, ideally in the *Sunday Times*. She explains that this is to build a foundation of high quality press while they work on the Sorrel Farm cook book over the coming year. Zoe looks as though she wants to sink into the floor when they discuss this, while Evelyn beams at the prospect, and Sadie is coolly confident. Then he's blown away when she says his name and mentions in front of the group that she and Evelyn have lined up an FT column interview with him for the following month. He didn't see that coming, but he'll take it. He'll take anything that helps the farm and gets him closer to her.

After the meeting, they all file back to the office. She walks ahead with Evelyn, Angus and Danny. Danny keeps up what looks like a steady patter of conversation before reluctantly parting ways with her at the door and heading away with Angus. Ned sits back down at his laptop. This is ridiculous. He has to do something; he can't remain in this limbo where he lets his feelings for her distract him from the job he's here to do. He has to take action. He stands and heads over to her. It's the strangest feeling, knowing a woman so little and yet feeling so beholden to her, wanting nothing more than to lie down next to her and put his arms around her and never, ever let her go.

~

Sadie licks her fingertip and rubs at a pen mark on the otherwise pristine white lacquered table. It's an attempt to distract herself from Danny, who's just delivered his usual stream of sexy grins and suggestive eye contact, despite keeping his conversation clean given Angus and Evelyn's proximity. He and Angus are both buoyant; it genuinely seems he enjoys his new role. She smiles inwardly. Just being with him buoys her up too; his dry wit and overt interest make her feel ten feet tall. Something's got to give on that front, and soon.

A shadow falls over her, and she looks up. Oh, no. It's Ned. He's fiddling with a biro.

'Yes?' she asks in her most off-putting tone.

‘Hi.’ He pulls the biro lid off and fits it back on again.

‘How can I help you?’ She knows that demeanour, and it’s the last thing she needs right now.

‘I wanted to say thank you for organising the FT interview.’

‘Not a problem.’ Her delivery is clipped and does nothing to encourage conversation. She looks at her screen.

‘Should I—do I need to do any prep for it?’

She looks up. ‘It should be straightforward. I’ll send you some past columns for reference. And I’ll ask Evelyn if there’s any angle she wants you to push regarding the farm.’

‘That would be great, thank you.’

‘Sure.’ She looks back at her screen, but she can feel him loitering. She’s losing patience now. ‘What?’

He hesitates. ‘A few of us are heading over to the Oast House for a quick drink this evening. I wondered if you’d like to come?’

The trouble is, his interest in her is written all over his face. He’ll never know how many times she’s had to bat away other Neds, whether she’s single or not. This happens all. The fucking. Time. It’s critical to set boundaries of steel. Don’t give an inch. No mixed messages. No explanations or caveats. It’s far kinder, and less painful for everyone concerned, if she’s crystal clear up front.

She looks up at him. ‘I would not.’ She maintains eye contact, waiting to confirm he’s got the message.

He blinks; he looks shell-shocked. He’s not unattractive; in fact, he’s a pretty good-looking guy. He just doesn’t have much else going for him. His clothes are typically awful today; the same boxy shirt and ill-fitting trousers as usual. He’s awkward and nerdy. He and Danny are night and day. Danny looks like all he thinks about is sex. This guy—well, suffice it to say it’s never going to happen.

He hasn't left yet. For fuck's sake. '*What?*' she asks again.

He's still struggling. 'Not the friendliest, are you?'

She sighs with ill-concealed frustration. 'And yet, here you still are.' *Subtext: please fuck off and stop bothering me.*

'Got it.' He holds up his hands in defeat. 'I'll leave you to your work, Princess Charmless.'

She almost laughs. How rude. Maybe he's not the pushover he looks. Cheeky fucker. At least he's got the message.

9

After what feels like an eternity, Evelyn gets a WhatsApp from Zoe, suggesting that they catch up for a coffee one day soon, after the lunch service. She accepts with relief. She can't hold Avery off forever, so Zoe's apparent willingness to engage is most welcome. They settle into a couple of old leather armchairs in a cosy corner of the Oast House. Zoe's changed out of her whites into a long, flowing scarlet skirt and a purple sweater. She's wrapped her braids up in a turban, also scarlet, and shot through with gold thread. The warm, vibrant tones look amazing on her. She's glowing, as usual, so when she tells Evelyn she hasn't been sleeping, it's a surprise.

'That's not like you.' Evelyn sips her green tea. Zoe's one of the least troubled souls she knows. 'What's up?'

Zoe folds her hands in her lap and cocks her head to one side. 'I don't like being insincere with my friends, and I feel I haven't been fair to you, Evie. I've been'—she stumbles over the English word—'disin*gen*uous.'

It's unlikely Zoe has an insincere bone in her body.

'How so, darling?' Evelyn asks. 'If anything, I feel I haven't been fair to you. I've had my own agenda and I've been trying to steamroll you into something you aren't comfortable with—'

'It's not that.' Zoe holds up her hand to interrupt. 'You're offering me an amazing opportunity. Amazing. It's every chef's dream, and I know you can get this for me—I should be so grateful. And instead I've been trying to make you feel bad for pushing me towards something I know will be good for all of us, when there's no way you could know why I'm so reluctant to take this step.'

Now that Zoe seems on the verge of opening up to her, Evelyn's curiosity is matched with a pang of guilt. She puts her hand on Zoe's and gives it a squeeze. 'You don't have to tell me, sweetie. It's none of my business.'

'I want to.' Zoe nods to drive home her point. 'I've wanted to for a while now. You've always been such a dear friend, but now you are with Angus, and the four of us are on this amazing adventure together, and—Angus and Jess both know about my past. I don't want to leave you out. It doesn't feel right.'

'Okay,' Evelyn says slowly. 'If you're sure you're comfortable opening up to me, then I'm honoured. But I'm a bit nervous now—has something bad happened to you?'

'Not bad, no.' Zoe smiles to herself. 'But crazy: you may think I'm crazy when I tell you. But it may also explain some things about me.'

Curiosity and nerves jostle for space within Evelyn. It's as though she's on the edge of a precipice, about to solve a mystery whose existence she was blithely unaware of until recently.

'No judgement, I promise.' She gives Zoe her warmest smile and her full attention.

Zoe exhales. '*Alors. Par où commencer*? Do you know, that when I was a young girl—twelve—I had a brain tumour?'

'No! How awful!'

'It was bad—I was in so much pain. So much time in hospital. The surgeons told my parents that the only chance for me to survive was with an operation to remove it, but it was extremely risky. It was such an impossible choice for them, but we made the decision as a family—me, and my parents, and my sister—that I would do it. I wanted to live.'

'Jesus.' Evelyn's head is already in her hands. She can't even conceive of how she would cope if Eddie was in that position.

'Anyway.' Zoe's voice gets quieter. 'I had the operation and—there was a complication. I don't understand all the details, but, for a couple of minutes—well, six minutes, actually—I was clinically dead. I died on the table.'

Emotion and horror floods Evelyn, and her hairs stand on end under her sweater, as she attempts to reconcile this statement with the fact that the woman uttering it is sitting right opposite her, in perfect health. All she can do is repeat the phrase: *You died?* It makes no sense at all.

'It's a very long story,' Zoe says. 'But yes. I had what in English they call an NDE—a near-death experience. In France we call it an EMI—*expérience de mort imminente.* My heart stopped beating, and I showed no brain function. The doctors gave up trying to resuscitate me, and they declared me dead. But before they were able to tell my parents, my heart restarted. I was still unconscious; I was under general anaesthetic. The doctors were so freaked out, they aborted the operation and closed me back up again.'

Evelyn stares at her in utter incredulity. Zoe's delivery is so matter-of-fact, and yet the story she's telling defies belief.

She has so many questions, but the first thing she blurts out is: 'So, what happened to the brain tumour?'

'It went away.' Zoe raises her arms balletically. 'Like—poof! It shrank over two weeks while I stayed in hospital. It just went away by itself.'

'Holy *shit*.' This tale is so insane that if anyone other than Zoe was recounting it, she'd call them a fantasist or a plain liar. She has a murky awareness of what near-death experiences are, but they've always been the realm of daytime TV, where odd-looking people describe tunnels of bright white lights. Speaking of which:

'Did you have any weird experiences? Like—bright lights, that sort of thing? Or did you not know anything had happened until you came around? You said you were unconscious.'

'Are you sure you want to know?' Zoe's tone is teasing, but her smile is celestial, and it makes Evelyn shiver.

'You can't stop there.' She tries to match Zoe's lightness of tone. 'I've never heard anything like this.'

Zoe leans forward. 'I was unconscious, as far as the surgeons were concerned. But, *ma chérie*, while I was supposedly dead, I had the most beautiful, infinite, profound experience of my *life*, and it altered me forever and nothing about my human existence has ever been the same since.'

A thought hits Evelyn; a sudden understanding that she's finally getting to the reason why Zoe is the way she is: otherworldly and unfettered by the daily shit that seems to bog everyone else down.

'Go on,' she says.

'I felt a wonderful sense of peace.' Zoe's face is dreamy. 'And a sense of... *knowing*. An instant, breathtaking understanding of what life, and death, and the human experience is all about, of what truly matters. And it's none of the stuff we obsess over on a daily basis. I understood that we are all connected by our souls, that our physical bodies are irrelevant, and that death is a thin veil that means very little, really. We continue to be connected to each other, whether we are on this physical plane or not. I had this download of comprehension, and at the same time I felt enveloped in an aura of very profound love and kindness, like I was safe, whether I decided to move forward, or go back.'

'Jesus,' Evelyn says again. She has no words to express how profound or incomprehensible this is. 'So—you believe you had a choice? To die or live?'

'Yes, but—at the same time, I knew which decision I was supposed to make. It wasn't my time yet. I understood that I should go back to this physical body, and to my family, and that no matter how long I lived, this other reality would always be waiting for me. It wasn't even that, actually—it was more an appreciation that this other realm would always be *there*, that it is around us all the time, even if we are not aware of it. And, I think there was a realisation, too, that if I went back, my physical ailments would vanish too.'

Evelyn is reeling from these revelations, revelations that are so enormous and weighty that she's struggling to digest them. Her tea gets cold as she asks Zoe question after question about what seems like a miraculous experience. They cover the fateful day itself: the joy and incredulity of her family and the surgical team in the fortnight that followed her procedure. More fascinating than the novelty factor of the inexplicable nature of Zoe's death and recovery themselves is the profound and lasting impact this has had on her. Zoe describes it as the instant and complete removal of fear.

'When you understand that there is nothing to fear from

death, because it's beautiful, and because it is not really a death, you have nothing left to fear in life,' she says. 'These days, I understand that we are all unique, beautiful, eternal beings, infinitely connected to each other and to the earth.'

'Do you think that's why you've got so passionate about nature?' Evelyn asks.

'It has definitely been helpful to me in finding a way to express this connectivity,' Zoe says. 'I see every form of life as the same expression of love, so I want to nurture plant and animal life and strengthen those connections. But it gives me comfort when I feel lonely, too.'

'How do you feel lonely, if you have this understanding—far better than most of us, it sounds like—that we're all connected?'

'The best way I can explain it is that when the veil was lifted, sometimes I feel as if I came down on the other side. People are so driven by fear and division; they cannot help it, but I struggle sometimes to connect when my world view is so far removed from theirs. They are so... *enlisés*—stuck in their worries?'

'Bogged down?'

'Exactly. They have a very different perspective than me. And that can be a wide bridge to cross.'

Evelyn can see that. People are drawn to Zoe because of her incredible energy, which is like nothing Evelyn's felt from anyone else, and yet her otherness does separate her from the crowd. It's fascinating to gain this backstory, even if the origins of Zoe's uniqueness are mind-blowing.

'I get that,' she tells her now. 'It must be frustrating. Is this why you're reluctant to share too much of yourself?' As she utters the words, she understands that this is precisely why Zoe's shied away from capturing her philosophy on paper.

'It is.' Zoe rubs her forehead. 'I can't separate my existential philosophy from my food, or farming, philosophy. I don't want it to be a distraction, and I don't want it to alienate me from the readers. I want them to invest in the ideas we share in the book, without feeling like a crazy woman is talking.'

'No one would call you crazy! But I understand; it's such a private thing you've told me. I can see why you're protective of it.'

'There's one more aspect I haven't shared.' Zoe squirms, her usual poise momentarily disturbed. 'Since the NDE, I've had a greater knowing about how the world works, and an understanding that time and space are not as linear as we see them to be. Sometimes, that means I know what will happen before it happens.'

'You're psychic?' Evelyn sits up straighter.

'Kind of. It's called clairvoyance. I understand information about my future. It is very selective. For example, I did not know that I would meet Jess, but I always had a sense of strong female energy. Mia gave me a clearer signal. She has always been in contact with me; I knew I would have her as my daughter when I was thirty-four.'

This is insane. Evelyn has always thought it odd that Jess went through IVF before Zoe, even though Zoe is a good six or seven years older than Jess.

'Is that why you waited?' she asks now. 'Is that why you let Jess go first, and get pregnant with Mike?'

'Yes.' Zoe smiles her beautiful smile. 'I was in no hurry. I knew Mia would come to me when she was supposed to. And Mikey was a beautiful surprise. I didn't see him in my future.'

Evelyn exhales. 'Holy shit. This is another level—I can't believe it.'

'It's a lot to take in. I'm sorry, Evie! I'm so pleased I can finally share it with you.'

'Thank you for trusting me with this,' Evelyn says. 'I promise you, I will never betray your confidence, or make you do anything you're not comfortable with. I assume Angus knows?'

'He does,' Zoe admits. 'We had so many pot-fuelled, late night talks about the meaning of life. You can imagine—two theology students. And Angus always had the best pot!'

That image makes Evelyn smile. 'I had a feeling he knew something, but he was very discreet. Phew.' Evelyn puts her head in her hands. 'My mind is officially blown. So, where does this leave us with the book?'

'I trust you, Evie. Now that you know everything, I will do as you think. I trust you to protect the parts of my story that are too heavy, and bizarre, and precious for a cookbook, but if you will help me distill my beliefs about the land into something you think people will respond to, then I will do it.'

10

When Evelyn gets home that evening, her mind is still racing. All afternoon, she's been asking herself what it would be like to have experienced what Zoe has and to view the world through that lens. She's done more than her fair share of yoga, meditation and gratitude practices, but this is another level of spirituality, and she's out of her depth. It's heavy shit, the realm of *bona fide* miracles, and it makes her feel—weird. She keeps thinking of Zoe, who she's always thought of as an extraordinary human being, but who, it turns out, has had a brush with eternity. Everything feels different, as if Zoe has successfully lifted that veil a fraction to show her a glimpse of what lies beyond the physical world that dominates her consciousness.

During supper with Eddie and Angus at the kitchen table, she's quiet. She's not distracted; she's the opposite. She's hyper-present, attune to every tiny, perfect detail. Einstein's words dance around her head.

There are only two ways to live your life. One is as though nothing is a miracle. The other is as though everything is a miracle.

Is this how Zoe lives every day? Is marvelling at everything instinctive for her, rather than a mindfulness chore? The soft, dark blonde hair spouting from Eddie's cow lick is magical; the fact that the three of them are sitting here, in a beautiful home with steaming bowls of prawn curry seems like the work of angels. She's been considering all afternoon what it would be like to live without fear, as Zoe does. There are some limits. Believing in an afterlife and the infinity of the soul is all very well, but it wouldn't help in the slightest if Eddie or Angus were ill or dying. That said, it's a damn sight better than believing in nothing but cruel randomness and seeing the human life-span as a cosmic blip.

'You okay?' Angus asks. He reaches over and squeezes her hand, and she smiles at him gratefully.

'Never better, darling.'

That evening, she savours her time with Eddie more than usual. Her phone goes away and she and Angus play a few rounds of Go Fish with him. When she puts him to bed, she listens to every precious thought that he sees fit to bestow upon her. She thinks of what Zoe said about Mia: that she knew her, or at least knew *of* her, before she was born. That makes her shiver. That she and Eddie were predestined to be together is a beautiful idea, but it messes with her head.

When she's kissed him goodnight a thousand times, she extricates herself from his warm little paws and makes her way down to Angus. He's sitting in the huge but wonderfully warm conservatory, which has retained the warmth of the afternoon sunshine. She clambers into his arms on the big sofa, and he kisses the top of her head.

'So,' she says into his chest, 'I had a long chat with Zoe

today, and she told me everything about—her past. Her near-death experience.'

'Oh, wow.' His breath is warm on her hair. 'How are you feeling about it all?'

'Mind-blown. Literally. It's hard to make sense of it.'

'I can imagine. I had years to come to terms with it, and it still blows my mind.'

'Do you think that's why she did theology at uni?'

'Definitely. She was looking for answers, but I don't think she found them at Oxford. So much of Western theology is dogma and doctrine. As far as I can see, she's found far more clarity by studying Eastern philosophies and spirituality.'

'How do you think she lives with something like that?'

He's silent for a moment before he speaks. 'Obviously I didn't know her before it happened, but it's an innate part of her, from what I can tell. That's what's struck me most, as an observer: we spent three years studying the minutiae of the world's greatest and most ancient religions, and yet I've understood more about what spirituality means from watching Zoe. She lives it. She goes about her daily life as if we're all connected to each other, and to everything on this earth, and to everything above us, whatever that may be. And it informs everything she does: her relationship with her wife, with her kids, and with nature. Whether or not you believe what happened to her is real, she's made it real.'

She shifts so her legs are across his, her entire body leaning into him.

'Do you believe what happened to her is real?' she asks him.

'Look.' He gestures before returning his hand to her shoulder. 'She's not stupid. She's read up on every aspect of this, and she's been pooh-poohed by doctors for decades. It's one of the reasons she's so hesitant to talk about it. She's been told time and again that what happened was a trick of the brain, that the feelings of bliss and interconnectedness can all be explained away by various parts of her brain shutting down during her trauma in surgery. And that may be. But those same doctors can't explain how her heart and brain function restarted after they'd ceased resuscitation efforts, and it also comes back to the point I just made: if she believes it was real, and if what she experienced was so transcendent that it's stayed with her since then and transformed her worldview, then *it's real*. There's nothing fake, or misguided, about it.'

'I don't know whether it's a blessing or a curse,' Evelyn says. 'To have the veil lifted like that, I mean. Sometimes I think ignorance is bliss.'

'Zoe sees it as a blessing—a privilege. It's simplified life no end for her; it's shown her what's important. Can you imagine what it would be like never to sweat the small stuff? She sees far more rhyme and reason to life than we do. She understands that seemingly cruel and senseless events carry meaning; I think she sees the patterns of nature and of humankind more clearly than we do. And she's far more accepting of what life throws at her—*far* more. Have you ever noticed how often she says *on verra bien*—we'll see?

'That's why the journey of this farm has been so incredible for her, and also for me, working alongside her. If you believe that everything on heaven and earth is interconnected, you're bound to love biodynamics! There've been countless times when I've wanted to intervene, when we've had creeping thistle on the rampage, or snails climbing all the fruit trees—you name it. And Zoe always persuades me to sit on my hands. She always says *on verra bien*. And she's always right. Nature finds a solution, or the creeping thistle ends up attracting a butterfly rampage... There's nothing like stepping back and letting nature do its thing to understand how perfectly, how intricately, the entire ecosystem works when we stay the fuck away.'

'I love that.' She glides her lips along the beginnings of stubble on his jaw. 'You know, she's put the book decision in my hands. And I'm so torn. The crass marketeer in me is drooling at the mileage we'd get from this angle in the press, but it's far more important that I protect Zoe, and in any case I don't want to muddy the message. But all that stuff you said at the end—that's really great. Maybe there's a way to build on that as background to Zoe's food philosophy, without spilling the beans on her past.'

'I think so.' He turns his head and kisses her, slowly, adoringly. 'Everything I've said—she can communicate it a million times better than me. You've heard her. She's spine-tingling when she gets going. There's no reason you can't tap into the unique perspective that she brings without divulging quite how she came upon this perspective. Books exist to alter mindsets and help us grow. My instinct is, you should keep the spiritual aspect light. Focus on the benefits of biodynamics and why it's the right way to farm, and the right way to eat.'

'That's what I've been proposing all along,' she points out. 'Zoe's got her knickers in a twist over nothing. She can easily front this book without giving away too much of herself, and she can weave her magic and spellbind her readers without spilling her secrets.'

'Precisely.' Angus' voice is muffled; his mouth moves slowly down her neck as he pulls the neck of her sweater away from her shoulder. If she's required to believe that life has rhyme and reason and patterns observable only to an enlightened view, then she can believe it easily, because the universe conspired to serve up Angus precisely as her marriage was ending. There's nowhere else she'd rather be. There's nowhere else she's supposed to be except here, with his lips on her skin.

'But *you*,' he continues, 'you blow my mind more than any near-death experience. I have my own *petite mort* every time I get near you. Let's go to bed.'

11

The next time Sadie sits down with Evelyn, Jess is in tow. She hasn't had much contact with Jess, but she liked her the moment she met her. She's a curvy, bouncy blonde with a vocabulary that would make an East End trader proud. She's the antithesis of her willowy, dark, soulful wife. That Jess and Zoe are such polar opposites, and yet appear so besotted with each other, makes Sadie inexplicably but supremely happy. These two give her hope for humankind and for relationships.

With the Harvest Festival a week away, Evelyn wants to update Jess on the preparations and the press attendance. Jess is technically the farm's Chief Operating Officer, but she's also in charge of the resort side of things, with Zoe running the food operation and Angus managing the farm. It's becoming clear that this place still operates like a family-run business, despite the structures that Evelyn's cash injection will allow them to put in place. It's more chaotic than Sadie would have expected, but somehow she loves this aspect. Sorrel Farm is a product of the colourful characters who run it, and it's all the more charming for it.

She sits with Jess and Evelyn in a cosy corner of the Oast House, perfect to catch the afternoon light. They work through the agenda and cover the journalists who've accepted an offer of rooms, what extra treatments and goodies they'll lay on for these guests, and what coverage they expect for the resort in which publications. Coordinating the Harvest Festival has been a fascinating lesson in the synergies between the various parts of the farm. Angus' team has designed the layout for the outdoor events, including farm tours and children's activities in one of the large barns. Zoe and the kitchen staff have produced a beautiful menu for the evening part of the proceedings, which most of the press will attend. The event is intended to showcase the farm's capabilities and attract corporate clients for its produce, but it's a perfect opportunity to remind the press that Sorrel Farm isn't just a summer resort but a delightful retreat for all seasons. To this end, they have an ambitious calendar of PR events leading right up to Christmas.

Update completed, Evelyn snaps her laptop shut. 'I've got to run. I'm trying to firm up sponsors for the Christmas soirée. I think Astrid Carmichael's going to do it.'

'Oooh.' Sadie exhales. Astrid Carmichael is a big London-based designer who's built a stunning brand around a romantic, old-world take on Britain. She's on her way to doing for the UK what Ralph Lauren has done for the US. Her clothes are exceptional, and extortionate. 'How did you get her? She's amazing.'

'We know each other socially, so...' Evelyn tails off. 'Sorrel Farm is the perfect backdrop for her winter collection.'

Of course they know each other socially. Sadie imagines them catching up at various exclusive fundraisers and fashion shows, both beautiful, elegant and at the top of their game. A frisson of ambition runs through her. This is what she wants for herself someday, an element of the success and impact that Evelyn has worked so hard for and yet wears so lightly.

'Nice one, Evie,' Jess tells her. 'Sadie, stay with me. It'd be good to catch up. Evie keeps you on a tight leash, from what I can see.'

Evelyn makes a face at Jess and smiles at Sadie, before leaving them to it.

'Settling in okay?' Jess asks. 'Evelyn treating you well?'

'She's amazing. I don't know where she gets her energy.'

'That woman is a fucking rockstar. She's saved this place. Just having her around is transformative.'

'How long have you two been friends?'

'Since the start of secondary school. A long time. We both turn forty next year—we'll have to do something to celebrate.'

No wonder Evelyn seems so settled here. She's a true part of the Sorrel Farm family. Having said that, she's been through so much this year that it's a testament to her resilience that she manages it all so well. Her divorce hasn't even been finalised yet, though she tells Sadie it's very close to being done.

'She deserves a celebration,' Sadie says now. 'You both do.'

'If she's not married by this time next year, I'll eat my hat.'

'You think? She and Angus are very sweet together.'

'Never have I seen a man so in love. And she's besotted, too. They've turned up for each other at just the right time. The timing couldn't have been more perfect. Life.' Jess shakes her head and looks down. 'Sometimes, when you think it's just senseless fucking chaos, it gives you a glimpse of the rhyme and reason behind it all. That's what Zoe would say, anyway.'

In that moment, Sadie decides she really, really likes Jess. She's a potty-mouthed cynic concealing a giant open heart.

'Be careful.' Jess shoots her a sideways glance. 'I reckon there's something in the water here. You'll be married and knocked up before you know it.'

'Oh God, I hope not.' Sadie is horrified.

Jess laughs. 'That would be my reaction, too. Evelyn's so in love, she thinks everyone should be. Are you single?'

'Yep. I broke up with someone this summer. We'd been together five years. So I think I'll give myself some breathing space for the time being.' She feels disingenuous saying this, but she doesn't actually want a relationship with Danny—just some very hot sex.

'Do yourself a favour,' Jess says. 'Keep the fact that you're single to yourself. You'll be beating them off with a stick otherwise.'

Sadie's expression must have shown how true that prophecy is, because Jess raises her eyebrows.

'Already beating them off? Want me or Evelyn to tell anyone to fuck off?'

'Don't worry.' Sadie smiles at her. 'I'm perfectly capable of doing that myself, and I already have, more or less.'

'I love it!' Jess slaps her thigh. 'I bet you have. I wouldn't want to be the guy who gets on the wrong side of you. Zoe used to get hit on so much when we were younger. Guys would see us together and assume we were just friends. She was always far too polite. You need to stand your ground. People are just too fucking well-mannered for their own good, aren't they? Especially in this country.'

'Amen. Even the guys are. I'm sorry; it's just not attractive.'

'Agreed,' Jess says. 'I never went for the nice guys, when I was younger. Bad boys were much more my thing.'

'You were with guys, before Zoe?' This is new information.

'Jesus, yes. Only guys. I'd never even considered being with a woman until I met Zoe. The only way I can describe it is that I got pulled into her force-field and there was no hope for me. She was the most extraordinary fucking human I'd ever met.'

Jess' face takes on a faraway expression and Sadie knows, without a shadow of a doubt, that she's never been privy to the emotions Jess is remembering right now. Lucky Jess and Zoe. Lucky Angus and Evelyn. Maybe there is something in the water here. But if there is, it's not something Sadie's ready for at this point in her life. She's here to work, to make a name for herself. If there's anything in the water here, she hopes it's success.

12

Angus and Zoe have clearly done something to please the weather gods. The weather is perfect, and Sorrel Farm dazzles the visitors who pour in all afternoon to celebrate the Harvest Festival.

At the kick-off of the evening part of the festivities, Sadie takes her seat at one of the long trestle tables in the Oast House with a couple of journalists. In her hand is a plate piled high with the most delicious looking food. Zoe and team have excelled themselves. The huge space buzzes as guests sit down to dinner. The management team have decided on a free-seating format, and the tables that fill the room are beautiful runways of pretty tableware, endless wild flowers and herbs in pots, vases and jam jars, and clusters of pastel-painted mini squashes and pumpkins. The effect is exactly what Evelyn intended: abundance and fertility. It's magical.

Opposite Sadie sit Nigel Coulter, a former colleague and eternal drinking buddy from the *Tribune*, and Valerie Drax, a senior staffer on the *Sunday Times Magazine*. Valerie is her target journalist for Evelyn's dream article: the feature on

Zoe. Valerie is therefore Sadie's new favourite person, although they've never met. Everything she does today is to impress Valerie. She's stalked her since she arrived early this afternoon. She's had a fag with her behind the hay barn, even though she gave up a couple of years ago. She's allowing Nigel to tag along because he's a big deal from where she sits now, but also because he's got her back. He knows she needs an *STM* feature to make her new boss fall in love with her, and he'll help her win Valerie over. Tonight, Valerie is staying in one of the most beautiful cottages on the farm.

She tops the journalists up with apple cider and pours herself a well-earned glass. They've cracked open the cider they bottled last year. She's held off most of the day, despite the free-flowing booze. It's her first major in-house press event, and she's determined that everything should go off beautifully. Evelyn, Jess, Zoe and Angus have worked so hard over the past month. She takes a sip of the cider: it's absolutely delicious, but tastes potent.

'About time, gorgeous,' drawls Nigel. 'You've been far too well-behaved today. Bottoms up.'

Valerie takes a bite of perfectly roasted butternut squash, and her eyes roll back in her head. 'Oh my God.' Her mouth is still full. 'This is sublime.'

'Isn't it? Everything has come straight from the land.' Sadie leans forward in her eagerness to pitch Zoe's food philosophy. 'Zoe works around what food is available. She sets the Garden Menu every morning based on what's ripe, and her team forages daily too. Those chanterelles weren't on the menu for today, but apparently some of the sous-chefs found a glut of them first thing this morning, so they've added them in. Zoe calls it communing with nature. She's from Provence, and her entire approach to eating can be summed up by this idea of *la communion*. You should hear her talk about it. It gives me goose-bumps.'

'You sound just like Angus,' says a voice behind her, and she starts. It's Danny, and his hand is on the back of the chair next to her. He's wearing the more wintry version of the Sorrel farm uniform—checked shirt, gilet and cargo pants—and he looks likes heaven.

'Is this seat free?' he asks, and Sadie spins back around to look at Valerie and Nigel. The red-blooded woman in her wants him right there, right next to her, but her inner PR maven is horrified. Danny's hotness will undoubtedly distract her from her charm offensive on Valerie. Unfortunately for her, Nigel and Valerie both fall over themselves to persuade Danny to join them. On their faces are matching looks of adoration and joy. She can't blame them. They're only human.

He sits and throws Sadie an infectious grin, which she tries not to reciprocate. He looks thrilled with himself. He pours himself a large glass of cider.

'You look stunning,' he tells her. 'Doesn't she look gorgeous?' he asks Nigel and Valerie, and they agree. This is mortifying. But it turns out, Danny is the perfect ally for her charm offensive. It quickly becomes clear that no one is more charming than Danny when he's on form. He manages to flirt equally with Sadie, Nigel and Valerie. The latter two are enthralled by his marketable brand of public school charisma and sheer hotness. He's tanned and a little sweaty. His shirt is slightly less than pristine, a sign that he's been toiling on the land today. It's all very on-brand for the farm and they all lean into his anecdotes and observations of the farm. He's witty and insightful. He's bloody perfect. And he adds that authenticity and perspective that Sadie wouldn't have been able to convey when selling Angus and

Zoe's philosophy to Valerie. His experience elsewhere, and the newness of his role here, makes him the perfect source to help Valerie judge what's so special about Sorrel Farm.

When Zoe, presumably urged on by Evelyn from somewhere in the wings, drops by in her chef's whites, Sadie almost laughs. It's all going too perfectly. Even in her whites, her beauty is other worldly. Danny's energy has buoyed them all up (as has the free-flowing cider), and the four of them are in a silly mood, but Zoe's appearance has a soothing effect on them. She's so radiant, so genuine and so passionate when she talks about the food she's created for today that they're eating out of the palm of her hand, as hypnotised by her as Sadie was when she first met her.

At some point in the evening, she notices Danny's arm draped casually across the back of her chair. When he wanders off to grab bowls of poached plums for them all, Nigel grabs Sadie's wrist across the table.

'Are you fucking that utter god?'

'No!' Sadie is mortified. She shoots a look at Valerie, whose face wears an amused half-smile.

'Well, you should.' He exchanges knowing glances with Valerie, who has somehow become his partner in matchmaking.

'Darling, if I wasn't an ancient hag with three grown-up children, I would pounce on that man so hard he wouldn't know what had hit him. He wants you. You're young and depressingly beautiful. Do me a favour. Fuck him, and tell me *all* about afterwards. Nigel and I will leave you two alone after pudding. Won't we, Nigel? I feel a bath in my divine cottage coming on.'

Sadie starts to sweat inside her denim midi-dress. She's not stupid; she's aware of Danny's intentions. She's *hyper*-aware. When he returns to the table, she's newly self-conscious, watching herself and him through the gaze of two Fleet Street hacks. Danny's oblivious to the conversation he missed, but his attention is solely on her. He's considerate, he laughs at her jokes and his arm is firmly back on her chair back. She's in that wonderful zone where she's so attracted to him that everything he does seems sexy. Just watching him put his spoon in his mouth turns her on. His hands are strong and lightly golden-haired with short, square nails. When he speaks, his mouth curls up over his straight white teeth and she wants to lick a line across them.

She eats her poached plums, enjoying how perfectly the spiced tartness of the fruit complements the rich custard. She takes her time, willing Nigel and Valerie to do the same and stay here in moral support. Of course, they seem hell-bent on doing just the opposite, and they make their excuses after coffee.

Valerie kisses Sadie on both cheeks. 'You're delightful, and so is Zoe. I'm sold. Give me a call during the week.' She pauses and lowers her voice. 'And remember. He's delightful too. I want *dirt*.'

When they've gone, Danny twists around in his chair to face Sadie. 'So. I've finally got you to myself.'

They're in a roomful of noisy, boisterous people, and yet it feels like he does have her to himself. Around them, the party is blurry, indistinct, while in front of her, she's aware of every detail of him. Everything in the last month has led them up to this point. She's tacitly encouraged him for weeks, and she's kidding herself if she thinks she's capable of withstanding him.

'Come outside with me.' Those ridiculous summer-blue eyes are guileless and pleading. 'I can't lay a finger on you in here.'

She attempts to hold herself together. 'Are you planning on laying a finger on me?'

'Ten of them, I hope.' He flashes her a grin. Alarm bells and desire jostle for headspace within her.

She should ask if he has a girlfriend. She should clarify this, for the girlfriend's sake as well as her own. She looks at his gorgeous features. He's still tanned from working outdoors in this glorious Indian summer. His hair is dirty gold and his teeth are blinding. He's smiling the sexiest, most hopeful smile, and he's smiling it at *her*. He keeps his eyes on her and his knuckles brush her thigh, right where her button-through dress falls open.

'I'm staying here tonight.' Back and forth go his knuckles. 'I have a room.'

'You're what? How did you wangle that? Aren't they full?'

'They had a last-minute cancellation. I have a friend in housekeeping.'

Of course he does.

He must see the uncertainty in her face. 'I cleared it with Angus. I'm doing him a massive favour, working the early shift tomorrow to get things straight after the party. I've been here for'—he looks at his watch—'over sixteen hours. So I've lost both my Saturday and Sunday lie-ins this week. He said it's fine as long as I pay the housekeeping fee. Saves me time in the morning.'

'You must be shattered. Time for that hot cocoa.'

'I told you the first day I met you.' His hand flips over and he massages her knee. 'I have no fucking inclination to drink hot cocoa. I have far better ways to wind down. I think you do, too.'

She really can't let him feel her up in a roomful of people. She really can't bear how much she wants his hand to travel up her leg. She slaps it off. It's so inevitable they'll sleep together that there's no point in messing around.

'I've been wanting to check out the bedrooms here,' she tells him, and she gets up and walks off. She looks behind her. 'You coming?'

She looks around the room as they leave. Huge chandeliers blazing. Tables lit dreamily by candlelight. The buzz of contented conversation and the heartwarming fragrance of good food. Tonight has been a success for the farm. Valerie seems to be on board. She can leave the event in good conscience. She glances at the beautiful man beside her, his smile confident and knowing, and her stomach flips in expectation. She's walking into this with eyes open. She doesn't want to know what his personal circumstances are. Right now, he wants her. He's wanted her for the past month. She's had monotonous monogamy for years. She deserves this. It's an act of self-love, really, to treat herself to Danny.

He opens the door leading out to the lobby and loos. He stands back to usher her through and follows behind her. Her coat is over her shoulders; his hand is on her lower back. A man comes out of the gents'. It's Ned. He brushes his hand through his hair and jolts when he sees them. When he looks at her, the expression on his face is sheer desolation. Devastation, even.

'Night, mate,' Danny says, unnecessarily cockily, and slaps him on the shoulder.

'Goodnight,' Ned mutters, and stumbles off.

She exits the main doors feeling slightly sick.

13

'Loser.' Danny glances backwards at Ned as they walk away from the Oast House. He says the word under his breath, but she hears it.

'You don't have to be a dick to him.'

'Tom says Lauren says he has a thing for you.'

This is too much. They're not in primary school any more. She stops and jabs him in the chest with her forefinger. 'Don't be so ridiculous. I'm not some fucking prize. I'm here with you right now because I choose to be, ok? Because I feel like having some fun with you. I can walk away at any second. So don't get cocky.'

The truth is, seeing Ned's face was a blow. She's caught him staring at her a couple of times since she declined his offer of drinks: not creepily, more forlornly. She has nothing against him. She's not interested, but neither does she want him to suffer unnecessarily. She'd rather just stay clear. But Danny's alpha-male gloating is not cool. She has to call him out on it.

'Relax.' He holds his hands up. 'I'm sorry. I'm on a bit of

a high, you know? The most beautiful woman is with me right now, and I'm fucking delighted. I'm well aware you hold all the power here. I'm putty in your hands, gorgeous.'

He takes a step towards her, and the momentary uncertainty on his face reassures her. This is a man who's never had to lift a finger to get a woman; it's heartening to know that she has even a semblance of control here. She lifts her face to his, but he shakes his head.

'Come on. Let's get you out of here. Believe me, you don't want any of your clients seeing what I'm about to do to you.'

He leads her along a gravel path to the old stables, which are now bedrooms. It's a still, moonlit night and remarkably peaceful now they're away from the Oast House. He unlocks a door on the ground floor and ushers her through to a large, pretty room. Warmth hits her, as does a heavenly botanical scent. The curtains have been drawn, and the lamps turned on. The room is dominated by a huge white bed, the covers turned back. She swallows.

Danny closes the door and they stare at each other for a moment. Then he takes a step towards her and wraps a hand around her neck and puts his mouth firmly on hers. As she reaches up to him, her coat slides off her shoulders onto the floor. She ignores it. He tastes of cider and spices and smoke. His lips are soft but his tongue is taut and rough with need. It twists in her mouth and the heat of it echoes in her groin. He moves her to the door and pushes her gently up against it with one hand while the other continues to pull her face as close to his as is humanly possible.

She wills herself to remember this moment. Sex with David was always excellent, but it had become predictable. She's had one very mediocre encounter since him, courtesy of Bumble. Since then she's been antsy and has tried very hard indeed to ignore the fact that she needs a good shag. Throwing herself into her new role has helped. But already she's uncoiling here, in this man's arms, in this unfamiliar hotel room. Already she can tell he's going to be good at this. His pretty looks have an edge of raw masculinity; the confident way he's handling her is tinged with real need. She wants him to take control, to consume her.

They make out against the door for a few more minutes, his erection insistent through their layers of clothing, his hands running up and down the sides of her breasts to her waist, hips, thighs. He pulls away and shoots her a dirty grin. He's trying to catch his breath. He looks like sin personified. He's *gorgeous* this close up. His blue eyes are almost all pupil and they flick down to her mouth.

'Fuck.' His thumbs trace the underwire of her bra over her dress before he releases her and takes a couple of steps backwards. 'You are so fucking sexy. Take off your dress.'

'Take off your shirt,' she retorts, but she starts unbuttoning. As he watches her, he unzips his gilet, undoes a couple of buttons on his shirt and pulls the rest of it over his head. He's answered her question. He does have builders' tan lines, but they're subtle, and his torso is still golden. It's also perfectly defined: dark blonde hair adorns his chest and his shoulders and arms are just beautiful. They're crying out to be stroked, nuzzled, kissed. She wants to run her nose and mouth along every curve of every muscle. He undoes the buckle of his belt, unzips his trousers and pulls them and his boxers down. This is a guy in a hurry. He hops to get them off without looking away from her performance.

When she's undone her buttons and her dress swings open like a coat, his face is a picture, contorted with want. He kisses her again, more greedily than before, and she gives the same back to him. The hairs on his stomach brush against her bare skin, and she arches her back as she gropes his neck, his shoulders, the velvety skin of his back. His hands go to her breasts, his fingers chafing at her nipples through the lace of her bra before sliding down her abdomen, dipping into her waist, and skimming over the fabric of her knickers. She's burning up already. They skim back up her body. He unhooks her bra and the front bobs up above her breasts, trapped by her dress. No matter. He bends and takes one nipple in his mouth, the other in his hand, and his free hand slips back down between her legs, pushing the fabric of her knickers aside. The collective pressure on all of her most erogenous zones is so insanely good that she's in danger of losing the plot altogether. She widens her stance to accommodate him and his fingers sink deeper.

This is no slow, methodical seduction. In another situation, she might be pissed off that a guy is rushing through the foreplay so quickly, but right now she's just as impatient as he is. His urgency is a huge turn-on; his desire is infectious. They're not even talking. His hands and mouth are everywhere, and she's vaguely aware that they're both moaning. She has him in her hand now and as she slides her fingers up and down his length, she whispers, *I need you.*

'You bet, gorgeous.' He tugs her dress down her arms and off. Her bra follows. He bends and peels off her knickers, kissing her stomach as he does, and she writhes in delight.

'Give me a sec.' He scrabbles on the floor for his cargo pants and pulls a wad of condoms out of the side pocket.

'So *that's* what those pockets are for.' She positions herself on the bed.

'They are very handy,' he acknowledges with a grin, and her attention is distracted by the glorious sight of him rolling on a condom. She scoots backwards on the bed and he kneels between her legs. His eyes are dark as he assesses her. She exhales. She bloody loves this moment. She's throbbing everywhere; even the skin on her arms is tingling in anticipation. She's on the precipice, and she's about to be put out of her misery by this gorgeous man and his heavenly, golden body.

As she watches him, he takes hold of her ankles and guides her legs back. She holds them up and he crouches over her, bracing on his hands. When he edges partially inside her and then plunges the rest of the way in, it's too much.

He grins at her, and then frowns in an attempt to control himself. She laughs.

'I've wanted you for weeks,' he tells her as he moves inside her.

'Me too,' she manages, but it's hard to say more when he's bearing down on her so perfectly heavily, and the angle of her legs is letting him reach so deep inside her. She's so close that she's not quite thinking clearly, and she's certainly too far gone to be self-conscious. And so she does what she's so used to doing with David; she puts her hands on her breasts and runs her thumbs and forefingers around her nipples, pinching them. It's a well-proven technique that practically doubles the intensity of her orgasms. Danny gives a choked laugh when he sees her. His eyes are on stilts and the poor guy looks fit to explode. He picks up his pace.

'Fucking hell!' The pain in his voice tells her he's losing control. 'I've *never* seen a better sight. Are you close?'

In answer, she pinches harder and allows the sublime, magnificent dam to burst as pleasure courses through her and she cries out. He keeps moving, and it's so, so perfect she cannot get enough. She wants the heat and the shock waves to keep rippling through her forever.

As she's subsiding, he lets go too, shuddering and slowing to a few long, deep thrusts. He pulls back to let her release her legs, and she stretches them out stiffly. He lowers himself onto her and wraps her in his arms and, between kisses, tells her exactly how amazing he found sex with her.

But after their breathing has returned to normal, and he's trailed his fingers up and down her back, over her bum, down her arms, he clears his throat.

'Do you want me to call you a cab? I mean, you're welcome to stay. It's just that I need to be up at five tomorrow...' His voice trails off and his eyes flick away from her face.

She stares at him. Wow. She knows a dismissal when she hears one. She'd assumed she would stay and enjoy this beautiful room with him, but he's not exactly rolling out the red carpet and in any case, she doesn't want anyone to spot her sneaking around the farm on a Sunday morning in the previous night's clothes.

'A cab would be great.' Her voice has no trace of emotion. 'I'll just get dressed.'

He averts his gaze as she attempts to pick up her discarded dress and underwear without bending over too much. She scuttles into the bathroom and dresses quickly, wiping the smudges of mascara from under her eyes with a flannel. Not until she has her coat firmly tied around her does she feel sufficiently armoured up to face him again.

He's found himself a robe, and he saunters over to her. His eyes are warm with admiration; he doesn't seem remotely bothered that he's just screwed her and is essentially kicking her out.

'That was fucking amazing.' He kisses her jaw. 'You're a marvel.' It's such a funny phrase, so old-fashioned and unsexy. Perhaps he learnt it at school? *Thanks for darning my socks, Matron. You're an absolute marvel.*

She's determined to play this cool. 'It was fun. I'll see you at work.'

She heads out into the cold, clear night to find this damn cab and pulls her coat collar up around her neck.

14

Sadie isn't sure what to think. She's essentially had smoking hot, no-strings-attached sex with a gorgeous guy. It was just what she needed. So she's not sure why she feels kind of… fragile. Unmoored. There was something brutally efficient about the whole encounter —she was in that room with him for just over half an hour. It felt transactional.

Of course it was transactional. They both got exactly what they came for. He was flattering, and attentive, and very enthusiastic. She can't blame him for wanting the bed to himself when he had an early start after such a long day. She tries to work out what has her feeling off kilter.

The most likely scenarios are these:

1. She's out of practice. She's been in a relationship for five years and she's forgotten how to do casual sex. The Bumble guy she slept didn't count, because she wasn't that into him. She needs to chill the fuck out.

2. Her ego is bruised. Danny's been all over her like a rash for weeks and has made no secret of how attractive he finds her. She knows he was *very* into her during the act

itself. It would have been gratifying had he been a little more clingy afterwards.

3. She's deflated. She can't deny the ongoing dalliance with Danny has been a welcome diversion, a sparkle in her day. Sexual tension is always at its hottest when it's unconsummated. She can't help but wonder if she's lost that now. It's always been abundantly clear what type of guy he is. Perhaps he'll move on to unchartered territories.

At work, their dynamic remains, confusingly, the same as before. She's filled with the usual excitement and dread of seeing him, a conflict familiar from her early twenties, especially if the person she pulled was a colleague. But he pops up mid-morning on Monday, ostensibly to see Jess, and settles himself on the edge of the table beside her chair. His smile is as dirty as ever, probably more so because she knows he knows what she looks like under the jeans and sweater she's wearing. There's an air of knowing in his eyes that wasn't there before.

She looks at him with new eyes too. She's never sure what's more intimate—knowing what someone looks like naked, or knowing what their face looks like when they come. When her gaze roves indulgently over his gorgeous features, her mind treats her to a rapid succession of heated flashbacks that make the muscles in her groin clench.

'You look incredible,' he tells her, his eyes dipping down her sweater. 'If only we could give housekeeping another call, eh?' As he gets up to leave, he bends over and whispers in her ear. 'I can't stop thinking about you on that bed.'

After a couple more encounters like this, she realises what he's doing. He's keeping her warm. He hasn't asked for her number, because he doesn't have to. She's a sitting duck—he knows exactly where to find her, and should the right opportunity present itself again, he'll give her the nudge.

What the appropriate feminist response is here is something she does *not* know. It's not clear whether she should feel put out that he's making such arrogant assumptions, or liberated by what's arguably an intoxicating situation: he still wants her, and if she lifts a finger, he'll come running for another fast and furious release. The only thing that is clear is he's not about to ask her out for a romantic dinner.

~

NED SHUFFLES the stack of papers as he stands by Lauren's desk. She's going to bind them in time for his meeting with Jess, Zoe, Angus and Evelyn. Jess and Zoe are old-school; they prefer printouts and a highlighter when going through the accounts. They've had a healthier third quarter than he could ever have conceived of a few short months ago, and this meeting is to summarise those results and sanity-check their forecasts for the fourth quarter.

She's talking to Sadie, but she holds her finger up to him to indicate that they're nearly done. Normally, he wouldn't hang around Sadie, though their working relationship has progressed to polite small-talk and accounting-based communications where necessary. He has a feeling that a couple of undiplomatic souls have told her he has the hots for her, and he would never want to make her feel uncomfortable. It would be utterly unprofessional and just plain unfair. She's shown nothing but complete disinterest in him and, more convincingly, he saw her leave the Harvest Festival with Danny last weekend. She looked lit up. He has to accept that they were likely going home together. The thought of that guy's hands on her makes him feel sick to his stomach. He doesn't have a chance with her, but Danny is too close to home. Since then, he's tried to give her a wide berth, but he really needs Lauren to get on this binding. He makes a herculean effort not to check out Sadie's slim, leggy figure in black trousers and a black polo neck.

The front door swings open. Lauren is the only person in the office who doesn't hot-desk; she has a reception station set up by the main door. A strikingly attractive brunette comes in. Her face is adorably flushed and her hair is damp. It must be raining outside. Under her open coat is the most perfect baby bump. One hand protectively cups the bump. There's something about her whole demeanour that speaks of home, of safety. Not like Princess Charmless standing next to him. An unwelcome image of Sadie, golden and radiantly pregnant, flashes into his mind and he blinks it away.

She looks at Lauren, still busy with Sadie, and turns to him tentatively.

He smiles at her. 'You ok there?'

'Hello.' She's sweet and shy. 'I'm looking for Danny Scott —I don't suppose you know where I can find him?'

Shit. His eyes flicker to her baby bump and back to her face. Everything makes sense in the worst possible way, and the fierce lick of anger that rises up in his chest makes him inhale sharply. He looks over at Sadie—he can't help it. She's already swivelled around at the sound of Danny's name and, as if in slow motion, he watches her clocking her and her bump in exactly the same way he's just done himself. Her eyes widen. He needs to do something. Now, for this poor woman's sake, as much as Sadie's.

He leaps into action.

'Of course. I'm sure we can track him down. He'll be out in the fields somewhere, most likely. I'm Ned, by the way.'

He's gabbling in a way he never does, but it seems critically important to keep her occupied and away from Sadie.

'Oh, thank you!' She takes the hand he offers. 'I'm Alice. I'm Danny's girlfriend.'

He doesn't look at Sadie, doesn't want to see the mental car-crash unfolding on her beautiful features. He gestures to a bench in the opposite direction.

'Have a seat, Alice.'

'I just want to drop off his lunch.' She holds up a carrier bag. 'He forgot it this morning. He'll be starving later.'

'Not a problem. I can put it in the fridge.' He gestures. 'Do you want to let him know you've left it in the office?'

He sees her out as quickly as possible, keeping up his cheery patter, and heads to the kitchen to bundle the carrier bag into the fridge. He's shaking. What a fucker. What a stupid fucking twat. What the *hell* is wrong with this guy? If Ned wasn't certain before that Sadie was involved with him, he knew it for sure as soon as he saw her reaction to Alice. He's messing Sadie around, and he's cheating on his beautiful, pregnant girlfriend. Ned can't get his head around who would actually do that. It's sickening. He thinks of Alice trudging over to the farm with her bump and her boyfriend's lunch, so worried he'll be hungry if she doesn't get it to him. Anger courses through his veins, as does the urge to punch the smug wanker in the face. What a piece of shit.

When he gets back from the fridge, Sadie and Lauren have vanished. Soon after, Sadie slinks back to her desk and slumps over her laptop. Her head is in her hands. He should be relieved that Danny's gone and ruined his chances with her, but instead he feels gutted for her. It's obvious she was unaware he had a pregnant girlfriend waiting in the wings. He goes back to the kitchen and makes two mugs of tea. One of them has two tea bags, and he mashes them with a spoon as best he can, adds a dribble of milk. He's seen her make her over-brewed tea often enough. It's a tiny thing, but he feels helpless. It's not his place to comfort her, but it's difficult to stand by and witness her distress.

He stops by where she's sitting. She's now chewing a fingernail and staring blindly at her screen.

'I was making tea, and I thought you might like one.' His tone is awkward. He puts the mug down next to her.

She looks up at him blankly. 'Thank you,' she says, 'for…' She waves her hand languidly towards the door.

He nods. 'Not a problem.' He'd like to ask her if she's ok, but he doesn't want to make her feel any more mortified than she already must be. The tea will have to do as a gesture of goodwill. He hurries back to his desk.

~

SADIE STARES AT THE TEA. It's just how she would make it. She could do with a glass of wine, but it's only eleven in the morning. Somewhere she registers that the tea is Ned's socially awkward gesture of sympathy and support. It's touching. But her brain is crowded with so many emotions that she's in danger of throwing her laptop across the fucking room. She is so furious with Danny for cheating on his pregnant, *beautiful* girlfriend—and for making her an unwitting accomplice—that she can't speak. It's so fucking low.

It's also plain nasty that she thought they were having sex as two equal, relatively unattached adults, when all the time he was in a serious relationship. It's a huge lie by omission and it shifts the power dynamic between them, somehow. She had no expectations from him, but to know he had this huge secret in his back pocket makes her feel violated. He pulled the wool right over her eyes.

She stays right at her desk until he turns up to take the bait: his lunch, packed by his adoring, oblivious girlfriend. She's facing away from the door, but she spots his back as he heads towards the kitchen. *Skulking* is the best way to describe how he's moving. No doubt he knows it's likely that she's onto him. He hasn't swung by her desk and his movements are hurried and furtive. He has on a wet mac. While he's at the far end of the room, locating his lunch bag, she grabs her coat from the back of her chair and scurries outside. It's a vile day: cold and wet. She pulls her hood over her hair.

He doesn't spot her when he comes out. She crosses her arms over her chest to keep warm.

'Danny.'

He turns around at the sound of her voice. Panic is written all over his face. He knows he's been cornered.

She strides over to him. 'You have a pregnant girlfriend. *Seriously?*'

He has the decency to look embarrassed. He puts his hands up. 'Can we do this somewhere more sheltered?'

There's a covered area around the far side of the offices. He takes her elbow to lead her there, and she pulls it away.

'Don't touch me.'

When they get out of the rain, she whirls around to face him.

'This had better be good. Go.' She's so angry she's shaking, and she feels lightheaded.

He sighs. 'Alice, my girlfriend, is pregnant, yes.'

Jesus. 'And you're sleeping around while she cooks your baby? Is this your first kid? Or are there more mini Dannys running around Kent?'

'God, no.' He—quite unjustifiably—looks morally outraged at the question. 'This is our first.'

'So what the hell do you think you're doing, cheating on her?'

'You're the only other person I've slept with, I promise.' Like that makes it any better. She raises her eyebrows and gives him her best contemptuous face. She's been told before it's effective. Sure enough, he shuffles his feet and looks at the ground.

'You didn't answer my question. *Why are you cheating on her?*'

'I don't expect you to understand. It's between me and Alice.'

'Now that you've fucked me, it's between you and me, too. Try me.'

'She's had a rough pregnancy—nausea; she's knackered all the time. It's been really tough on her, but on me too. She doesn't want to have sex, and I've been going out of my mind. And then you walked in on my first day, and I just thought *holy fuck*. You're so gorgeous, and you feel a world away from my home life.'

It's odd how quickly she's stopped finding him attractive. Now he just looks pathetic, and that is not a turn on. He sounds like a miserable, whiny child. For fuck's sake.

'You're having a kid together. You think your home life is going to get better when it's born? It's not. Presumably, this is what you both wanted, and I'm sure she didn't sign up for nine months of puking. So why you can't keep it in your pants for her, I'm not sure.'

'I know you're right, and I feel like shit about it. But she has no idea about us, and I'd like to think I'm a nicer boyfriend to her now that I've met some of my own needs.'

That actually makes her burst out laughing. He's managed to couch his need to get laid in psychobabble. He's beyond a joke.

He blusters on. 'I also feel really bad about misleading you. I think you're amazing, and I'm sorry I'm not in a position to give you anything… more. Are you ok?'

If she could breathe fire on this guy right now and watch him go up in flames, she would. She squares her shoulders and looks him in the eye.

'Believe me, I'm fine. And I want absolutely nothing more from you. Stay. The fuck. Away from me.'

~

AS HER ANGER at Danny settles into a steady smoulder, Sadie unearths another, less welcome emotion: self-disgust. It's been easy to retain the moral high ground with him, to play the oblivious victim. But she's been thinking back to Lauren's words of caution when she and Danny first met: *Tom said he mentioned a girlfriend*. Lauren never came up with any further colour, and Sadie didn't push. She didn't want to know, and when she went to that hotel room with him she deliberately opted not to ask him.

She as good as knew he had a girlfriend, but she forged ahead anyway because she had her own agenda: she wanted him, and she wasn't going to let any inconvenient truths surface and derail her. It's likely that even if she'd asked him, he wouldn't have admitted to a *pregnant* girlfriend; he would have fudged it and admitted to having someone in his life. In that scenario, if she's honest with herself, she would have gone ahead and slept with him anyway. In her mind there are degrees of wrongdoing, and she would quite happily have overlooked his faceless girlfriend in the heat of the moment, while now she feels justified in judging him for cheating. Who the expert is on where the line should be, she's not sure.

She's always done this, if she's honest. She's always pushed on with her own agenda, both at work and in love. David was seeing someone, albeit casually, when Sadie waltzed in and dazzled him. It wasn't hard. She's always been aware of her power to attract men, and because it's a power that comes easily, she hasn't given it the respect it warrants. She gives little thought to the consequences for the other women she tramples on.

Likewise at work. The cover feature she wrote on Evelyn for the *Tribune*'s Sunday supplement should have gone to a more senior staffer, but because she'd initiated contact with Evelyn, she fought tooth and nail to hang onto that piece. It pissed plenty of people off, but it was a huge step forward professionally and ultimately resulted in Evelyn poaching her.

That the end justifies the means is a philosophy she adheres to, consciously or not. She stands up for what she wants and she does everything in her power to get it. Usually, she measures her success by the extent to which she hits her target. But this time, her success has come back to bite her in the arse. She got Danny, and in doing so she could have jeopardised the happiness of some poor woman who has years of history with him and has made the ultimate commitment to a future with him by choosing to have his child.

The fact that this woman's character judgement is clearly awful is a moot point—Sadie fell for his charms too, after all. Seeing Alice in the flesh, complete with a beautiful baby bump, has scared the hell out of her. What she thinks of as a game, a bit of fun, turned alarmingly real when she walked through the office door.

It's the wake-up call she needed. No more. She has a feeling everyone in the office will know pretty soon. This kind of gossip is too good to ignore. In the days that follow Alice's appearance, gazing into bottomless cups of tea, she makes a decision. She will behave herself, and she will keep her head down. No more work flings. No more blinkered, self-serving stunts whose only relevant variable is how far they advance whatever agenda she has. Journalism has always been a cut-throat world, but here she's in a bubble, surrounded by decent people (with one glaring exception) and she'll use them as her moral compass. She'll rely on her skills and on hard work, she'll keep her head down, and she'll behave with the integrity she sees modelled around her. She's learnt her lesson.

15

This sunny Saturday, the kitchen garden at Sorrel Farm has an array of various-sized volunteers fully gloved up and harvesting potatoes by hand. The kitchen garden is an overflow of the walled garden, a six-acre field behind the back wall with raised beds. Angus has designed these beds so all the produce can be harvested without digging. Using a no-dig method has many benefits, but the primary aim is to improve the soil quality by allowing hardworking worms, fungi and bacteria to thrive without disturbance. They're in the process of turning another nearby field into a similar kitchen garden, thanks to the recent supplier contract from Seb Macleod limited, and the interest from other restaurants and hotels that's starting to build on the back of it.

He surveys his little team. The kids are doing brilliantly. His sons, Hector and Alastair, are both home from uni, and it's his weekend to have them. It's the first time they've stayed overnight at Belvedere; Eddie's been on cloud nine since they arrived. Eddie is beavering away too, competing against the teenagers, but Jess and Zoe's kids, Mike and Mia, are the most productive farmers here: they're old hands at this. They've been helping out on the farm since they were tiny. Mike's showing Eddie how to unearth the potatoes from the soft soil with his gloved hands and gently brush them off before putting them in the baskets.

Angus exhales. They're all getting on; everyone looks content and productive. Eddie has the glow of satisfaction that comes from such a palpably productive job. Since getting together with Evelyn, and particularly since they've moved in together, he's been consciously including Eddie in the group of kids for whom he provides some sort of father-figure services. Seb's a great dad, but he only sees Eddie every other weekend, and he's rebuilding his food empire without Evelyn as well as working on his newish relationship with Gino. Eddie needs an adult male who's on hand to deal with any of that stuff that boys need as they grow up, and Angus is intent on fulfilling that role as much as he can without treading on Seb's toes.

It's a role he's enacted for years with Mike and Mia. As one of Zoe's closest and oldest friends, it's Mia he's godfather to, but he's always aware that Mike may feel the lack of a permanent dad about the place. There's no treading on any toes here: Luke, who donated the sperm for both kids and is another old friend of Jess and Zoe, has a hands-off relationship with them both—he's a busy paediatric surgeon in Birmingham. Jess and Zoe have always encouraged Angus' involvement in their kids' lives, to an extent that has been the butt of many jokes. Jess is particularly paranoid that Mike and Mia are suffering from the absence of a proper, at-home father-figure. It's nonsense—they're the best-adjusted, most polite children he knows—but he loves being Uncle Angus.

Ironically, it's Hector and Alastair he worries about the

least. They were both away at boarding school when Audrey left him for a stockbroker who works more regular hours and 'sees her more fully'. Now they're in their third and second years at university respectively, and their focus has very much shifted from their home life to their intense university experiences. They began withdrawing from their parents in that cruel but inevitable way that teenage boys have before he and Audrey split. He knows the next decade will be the lost years, when they pretty much ignore their parents until they have babies of their own and rush back to the nest for support. Once again, he thanks whoever's up there for sending him Evelyn and Eddie.

The woman herself appears in the vegetable patch through the back door of the walled garden. She's wearing a brand new Barbour that needs to be worn in, though he can't imagine the brand would complain if they saw her; she looks like a very glossy advert as she tosses her beautiful chestnut hair back and gives him the full wattage of her breathtaking smile. For the millionth time, he shakes himself and vows to make it official between them.

Eddie's up off his knees and tearing across the grass as soon as he spots her. 'Mummy! I've picked *forty two* potatoes so far!'

He can't hear her reply, but she stoops and squeezes him tightly, the two of them forming a perfect tableau, back-lit against the bright sky. When she makes her way over to Angus, he bends his head and kisses her on her ravishing, soft mouth. It's a kid-friendly kiss, but her eyes are dancing as they pull away.

'So, handsome,' she says, 'how's it going with the little chain gang here?'

'They're doing great.' He wraps his arm around her

shoulders and she leans into him. 'I may never have to pay for labour again.'

'Excellent.' She looks up at him. 'I was watching you guys for a few minutes before you saw me. I have to say, it's given me an idea.'

~

OVER A LIVELY SATURDAY evening supper back at Belvedere later, she outlines her idea, but not before Eddie has impressed them all with the staggering array of potato-and-soil-related trivia he's absorbed today. It's been percolating while she was cooking, taking shape in an exciting way.

'Do you ever do school trips to the farm?' she asks, once the chicken tray-bake has been doled out.

Angus shrugs. 'We've done a few ad hoc ones, mainly with local primary schools. I'd love to do more, but it involves a lot of organisation.'

'Is organisation the main obstacle, rather than money?'

'It's a matter of time, really. There's so much back-and-forth with the schools to organise. We have to make sure any of the team here who interact with the kids are DBS checked. And most state primaries don't have budget for coach trips, so they limit their trips to where they can use public transport. Obviously, it's hard to get them out to the farm.'

'Hmm.' Evelyn sips at her wine. Just as she thought.

He looks at her. 'What are you thinking?'

'I'm wondering about putting a charitable programme in place. Look at how much Eddie picked up today, just by spending a few hours on one crop. I mean, you guys are lucky enough to have grown up with a dad who's a farmer.' She gestures at Hector and Alastair. 'But Eddie's a city kid.

Okay, he's learnt a lot about nutrition from Seb and me, but it's being hands on with the land that gets him really excited and inspired.'

Angus pours out some claret for her and his boys. 'You don't need to convince me. I believe all children should spend as much time outdoors as possible. What kind of scope are you thinking? Local schools?'

'For starters, maybe,' Evelyn says, 'but we're so accessible from London; it would be great to set up programmes for schools in built-up areas: Tower Hamlets—even Croydon and some of the suburban parts of north Kent. What would we need, apart from transport?'

'It needs to be educational,' Hector chips in. 'It's great to offer these kids a good run around at the farm, but you have an opportunity to sell them on the size of the environmental crisis facing us all. Use it as an opportunity to recruit your next generation of eco-warriors.'

'He's right,' Angus says. 'Ideally, we run it as a structured educational programme. We'd need a couple of qualified educational officers from outside the Sorrel Farm team, and probably a schools liaison person to manage the relationships and the logistics.'

'You know what would be cool?' Alastair asks. 'If you can make it an ongoing thing. Maybe you offer one trip each term for each school, or year group. That means the same kids come three times over the course of the academic year; they'd get a far better idea of the farming cycle that way and they'd learn totally different things each time.'

'I love that idea.' She can feel her excitement mounting, and she has a new rush of affection for these gorgeous, engaged young men Angus has raised so well. 'There's so much scope here to do something really exciting.'

Angus leans over and squeezes her hand. The expression on his face is one of amusement and affection. He knows this side of her, the side that burns with an idea once it takes hold. 'Where does the funding come from? I don't think the farm could support this right now.'

'No, not at all.' This is the best bit—she can finance this easily. 'It's something I'd like to fund, though we can do it under the branding of the farm. I've been looking for a charitable project to kick-start. I reckon Seb might be game, too. This is right up his street.'

The more she thinks about it, the more the warm glow of purpose mounts in her. She'll raise it with the management team at the Monday meeting. This could be huge—a chance to build on everything that Sorrel Farm stands for and spread the environmental lessons they've all learnt far beyond the converted elite of their own generation. The farm's legacy won't just lie in the ecosystems they create, but in the imaginations they capture, imaginations that are sorely needed if biodynamics are to have a future.

16

The *Financial Times* journalist, Nithya, is beautiful. She's tiny and glossy, long hair tumbling over her neat suit in shiny black waves. Her huge, dark eyes sparkle at Ned when he enters the room. Her mouth is a glossy red rosebud, but right now it's stretched into a dazzling smile as she holds out her hand to him. When she introduces herself, it's in a polished, East coast American accent, and immediately he's transported back to college, to his happy place. She's the picture of American good health and great dentistry.

Unfortunately, next to Sadie, she looks like a cartoon character compared to fine art. Sadie is washed out today. There are shadows under her eyes and ill-concealed boredom is plastered on her face. He was surprised when she told him she'd lined up this interview. She makes it clear his role is of no interest to her. He suspects Evelyn's behind this coup. Sadie's all in black and her usual gold jewellery glints on her wrists and at her neck. Her fine-knit polo neck skims her body so snugly it's almost unbearable. Her hair is scraped back, and she makes Nithya's healthy, vibrant beauty look overdone, commercialised. Every time he looks at Sadie, he wishes he was a painter.

When they're settled in the space Sadie has chosen—a quiet corner of the mezzanine in the Oast House—Nithya explains to him that she'll kick off with some background questions.

'Where did you grow up?' she asks.

'Around here, when I was younger. I went to the local grammar school. Then Berkshire, to a sixth form college. My dad was in the army, and when I was sixteen, he took up a teaching position at Sandhurst. He's still there, putting the fear of God into the new recruits.'

Nithya rewards him with a radiant smile. 'From grammar school in Kent to undergrad at Princeton. That's some move.'

Sadie sits up straighter and something flickers in her eyes—interest, perhaps. He keeps his focus on Nithya, who's obviously done some research on him already, and shrugs.

'I got lucky—swim scholarship to Princeton. My family could never have afforded it otherwise.'

Nithya is still beaming at him. 'Princeton is my *alma mater,* too. I miss it every day.'

'No way!' he says. A handful of his college friends made it over here, but most are stateside. It's always a pleasure to find people to reminisce with. 'When did you graduate?'

They shoot the breeze on Princeton for a few minutes. She's six years younger than him, so they didn't overlap, but they both majored in Economics.

'Still, a swim scholarship is extremely impressive.' She puts her arms flat on the table and leans forward. 'I can't even imagine what standard you were at to have won one. You must be an amazing athlete.'

Is she flirting with him? Sadie narrows her eyes; he

suspects she doesn't approve of journalists and interviewees going off track.

He laughs awkwardly. 'Not anymore, sadly. A sedentary job will do that to you. But they were good times.'

'So.' She taps her chin with her pen. 'Then back here, to Deloitte's?'

'Yes. That's where I trained as a Chartered Accountant.'

'And what prompted the decision to move in-house?'

'I did a decade there. It was great fun, but when you're always being seconded out to clients, you lose that sense of belonging. I got sick of swooping in and out of companies. I wanted to build something.'

Nithya sips her coffee daintily. She's like a little doll. 'What was it about Sorrel Farm that appealed?'

'I got head-hunted for the role, but it was exactly what I was looking for. A worthy enterprise, focused on doing good by the planet. Diverse revenue streams, which made things far more interesting for me. Plenty of opportunities for the business but a challenging balance sheet and the best team of people I've ever had the good fortune to meet.'

It's true. Sorrel Farm is a magical place to call his office, but really, it's the people who inspire him the most. Jess, Zoe and Angus are three of the most genuine, hardworking people he knows. And he's rapidly become a huge fan of Evelyn since she came on board, saved their arses, and began to whip them all into shape.

'This coffee is insane,' Nithya says. 'You guys are super lucky to work here. It sure beats the City.' She casts her eyes around the room and Ned sees her take in the plush sofas on the mezzanine level and the view over the railings, down to the main part of the Oast House. Delicious smells of breakfast still waft up from the kitchen, and the air tinkles with conversation. Thanks to the press attention Evelyn has attracted since the summer, the place is far busier during the day with local mums and entrepreneurs.

'How are you finding it, Sadie?' she continues. 'You've only been here a few weeks, no?'

Sadie looks up from mashing the tea bag in her little teapot. She pops the lid back on and pours tea so over-brewed that it resembles tar into her cup. It looks revolting.

'Nearly two months,' she says. 'And it's gorgeous. I'm not sold on living out of London yet, but the farm itself is certainly a very inspiring place to work. And I agree with everything Ned said. The management team is amazing. With people like that, you just want to work hard for them.'

She's not only volunteered information, but she's actually agreed with him. His shock must show on his face, for she gives him a little smile as if to say *see? I can be nice when I want to be.* There's too fleeting a glimpse of her dimples when she smiles.

'That's always good to hear.' Nithya fiddles with the voice recorder. 'I'm super jealous. How has your role changed since Evelyn Macleod came on board, Ned?'

He sits up straighter. 'It's got far more exciting,' he admits. 'For many companies of our size, the Finance Director role can be a juggling game, an endless dance to manage cash flow. You end up playing defence, focused on keeping the lights on rather than the opportunities. We've always felt strongly that there is so much potential for growth at Sorrel Farm, on both the farming side and the resort side.

'Evelyn's investment has allowed us to shift from defence to offence, and she's also kick-started new revenue streams for us: since we partnered with Seb Macleod Limited as a produce supplier, supplying enterprises with food is now a division in its own right. She's opening new doors for us, she's given us the liquidity to go after these opportunities, and her involvement has also boosted the capacity rates of our rooms and leisure club memberships. So the underlying business is healthier and more self-sufficient. It's a really exciting stage in our journey.'

'If you've read the column, you'll know I ask every FD this. What does the FD role mean to you, particularly in the context of your company?'

'I'm a facilitator, plain and simple.' He leans forward and smiles at Nithya. 'Yes, I oversee the budgets, and I have a view on every number that goes into our accounts. But Jess and Zoe have a vision, and I'm here to facilitate that vision in a way that is operationally and financially efficient. They're the architects; I'm the structural engineer. Can we do what we want to do on a cost base that makes it worthwhile? And can we finance that building work with capital that doesn't cost the earth? My job is to build a funnel that maximises the financial output of what the rest of the management team puts in.'

~

SADIE IS HUNGOVER. She finally went over to Evelyn's last night to check the new pad out while Angus met up with some friends at the pub. She knows the level at which Evelyn operates; she's seen the spreads of her old London house in *Food* magazine and *World of Interiors*. But what this new place lacks so far in sheer Holland Park gloss, it makes up for in size and charm. It's breathtaking. She watched Evelyn make an excellent curry from scratch while wearing head-to-toe Chanel. Handling turmeric while in Chanel should be illegal. They ate the curry at the large wooden table in Evelyn's new kitchen while Eddie ran around the house. He's a sweet little boy—gorgeous looking, like his famous father.

It was too dark to see the beautiful gardens properly, but she did get a peek inside Evelyn's dressing room, and it surpassed her wildest dreams. Evelyn claimed it would all be overhauled, with specially lit rails to display her shoes, but the stacks of boxes with designer names on them gave her goosebumps. She'll get Zoe on the cover of the *Sunday Times Magazine* and she'll earn that hour of playtime with Evelyn's clothes if it kills her. Meanwhile, she's lucky to have a boss who's so gorgeous, interesting and fun to drink with, while also being inspiring as hell.

She's been expecting this interview to be dull as ditch-water, hence the caffeine overload. Her tea bag is one of those fancy drawstring ones, stuffed full of some deliciously fragrant loose tea. She mashes it to within an inch of its life before pouring herself a cup. To her surprise, though, the whole session is proving more intriguing than she would have expected.

First, Nithya clearly has the hots for Ned. She's a gorgeous, glossy American, even though she's wearing a skirt suit that's so conservative, it's got to be Brooks Brothers. She must have been a banker in a previous life. Second, Ned is looking less offensive than usual: he's traded in his bulky, boxy shirts and diaper-butt chinos for a well-cut navy suit and tie. The vertical lines work well on him, and the suit gives him gravitas.

The biggest surprise, though, is that what comes out of his mouth is not boring at all. Not even in the slightest. On the contrary, he's smart, thought-provoking and self-deprecating. Admittedly, she's never given the farm's finances a second's thought before, but Ned makes the role sound fascinating. Reading between the lines of his self-deprecating answers, it's clear he's the quiet operator of the nerve-centre that allows them all to go about their business. She wouldn't even mind hearing more about that side of things. She's simultaneously grateful that Ned's getting a chance to tell the farm's story from this angle, and ashamed that she'd dismissed it as far from newsworthy.

Ned and Nithya get more technical. Evelyn had Sadie advise Nithya ahead of time that Ned wouldn't be discussing numbers: as a private company, they have no obligation to disclose their financials. But they geek out on growth rates, optimal capital structures for hospitality businesses, CapEx projections, whatever they are, and operational details.

As they do, her mind wanders. She's never seen Ned so animated. Nithya's clearly hanging on every word he says, and it brings him out of his shell. He seems pretty quiet in the office—she's certainly never aware of his presence—but now he's authoritative, and his enthusiasm for the business is infectious. Her gaze wanders too: it sweeps over Nithya's carefully waved hair (she has annoyingly good hair) and lingers on Ned's face. He's lit up, and his eyes flash when he makes a point in a way that's bizarrely attractive. He also has a captivating mouth. It's particularly captivating when he flashes Nithya a shy, unexpected grin. Maybe both of them had their dental work done stateside.

He has a habit of pushing his hair back from his face when he talks. She's not sure why he bothers; it falls straight back down again. Maybe he needs a hairband, like a Nineties David Beckham. Or a haircut. But the thing that really gets her is his freckle. A perfect little freckle sits bang in the middle of his right cheek. There's something about it that makes her stomach hurt. She has the unwelcome realisation that she'd like to touch that freckle. And as for the swim scholarship—bloody hell, that's impressive.

A hazy recollection surfaces: Lauren mentioned something about him swimming. It's clear she's underestimated this guy.

After they wrap up the interview and walk Nithya to her Uber, they head over to the office. This is the most time she's spent in his company and it feels awkward. She hugs her notebook to her middle.

'You did well.' She keeps her tone bright, forthright. It's important to give management feedback on how they perform with the press, and besides, he deserves to know. 'That was a good interview. I can tell she was happy with it. Well done.'

He blinks as if he's in shock. 'Oh. Thanks. I'm glad you think so. I don't do much press—I didn't really know what she was after.'

'It was interesting, what you had to say. We should look into getting more exposure for you, especially in the financial press. I can get on it.'

He holds the door open for her and gives her one of those shy smiles he rewarded Nithya with earlier. He's like a different person when he smiles. Being on the receiving end is a delight. 'Sure,' he says. 'Anything that helps the farm.'

She's surprisingly keen to prolong their moment together. 'I didn't know you went to Princeton. That must have been an experience.'

He shrugs. 'Best years of my life.'

'Were you a nerd or a jock?' She's careful to keep her tone bantering rather than flirtatious.

He grins, but looks surprised that she's voluntarily pursuing a conversation with him. Well, why shouldn't she make a bit of effort with her colleagues, get to know them better? 'It won't surprise you to hear I was definitely a nerd,' he says. 'Total geek. Although... being on the swim squad helped with my disguise—it got me into a good fraternity. So I guess I got the best of both worlds.'

There's a hint of an American accent when he says *I guess.* It's a glimpse of his younger self: smart, athletic and personable enough to hold his own in the hallowed halls of the Ivy League. It's a welcome insight. Ned epitomises the concept of still waters running deep. She doesn't doubt that currents run under his surface that people who dismiss him out of hand—people like her—can easily miss. She resolves to get to know him better.

She hasn't been back at her desk half an hour when an effusive WhatsApp message from Nithya comes through.

Hey! That was such a fun interview! Thank you for setting it up! Pls send me the headshot of Ned when it comes through. Thanks!!!

Then:

Also. Can you send me his email? I'd like to thank him in person and also ask him out for a drink (I thought he was super cute! And we have a lot in common...) <winking face emoji>.

For fuck's sake, thinks Sadie, as she copies Ned's email address into a message to send to Nithya. She's not sure what's got her back up. They're both finance geeks; they'd have a ball together talking about balance sheets and cash flow. It's because he's a part of the Sorrel Farm family, she tells herself. No matter how dull and nerdy he is, she still objects to someone swanning in from London and trying to snap him up.

When Clara sends the headshot through, she opens it to check it's appropriate for the FT. Clara's taken it in the courtyard. He's back-lit against the watery autumn sunshine. He's managed to keep his hair off his face, and he has a half-smile that looks wise and authoritative. His eyes are kind. She puts a fingertip to where his freckle sits on her monitor before hastily closing the image and forwarding on the email to Nithya.

The journalist replies on WhatsApp later that evening.

Hey Sadie! Thanks for the headshot—cute pic! So I bit the bullet and asked him out but sadly he's seeing someone <sad face emoji>! No surprise really. Will shout when I get a go-live date for the column! Nx

He's taken. Hmm. As Nithya says, no surprise really. It's good that he's moved on from her. In any case, she's done enough damage with her first foray into the menfolk of Sorrel Farm to stay well clear from now on, especially of ones that are taken.

17

That employees get half-price spa treatments is yet another reason to love working for Sorrel Farm. Sadie's just had a post-work pedicure, and she wiggles her red-painted toes admiringly as she settles onto a lounger by the indoor pool. She and Lauren are wrapped in fluffy white Sorrel Farm robes, plastic glasses of white wine in hand. Lauren has had a massage and is unlikely to hit the pool; she says she doesn't want to wash all those gorgeous essential oils off her skin. Sadie could be persuaded, though.

It's tropical in here. She unties the robe and lets it fall open, shimmying her arms out of it. She has on her favourite black one-piece, the one with an indecent slit down the front. Black is definitely the easiest colour to pull off if you have to expose your winter skin in swimwear. That's better. The warm air caresses her skin as she looks around. It's a crime she hasn't been here before now.

The space is breathtaking. The lights have been dimmed for the evening, and someone has lit candles inside the hurricane lanterns dotted all around the room: small ones on the tables and huge freestanding ones on the tiles. The pool glows aqua and the reflection of the lights plays on the vaulted glass roof of the orangery. Abundant ferns and palms in huge terracotta pots give the room a Harbour Island feel, and soothing meditation music plays. It's womb-like—a world away from the freezing evening outside. She may have to come here every night after work until spring arrives. It's such a joy to shed her clothes and yet feel so warm.

There are two more women reclining on beds at the far end of the room, and a swimmer cuts powerfully through the water, his bullet-like progress hypnotic. Otherwise, they have the place to themselves. Sadie lies back on her lounger and sighs with pleasure. Its mattress is bed-level comfortable and covered in cosy terry towelling. She takes a sip of chilled Sancerre. This is the life. *This* is why she moved to Kent. It beats standing in some grimy pub in Soho or Covent Garden after work, that's for sure.

'I may even get in the pool,' she tells Lauren, stretching her legs out languorously. 'After that lunatic has finished.'

She nods at the human bullet. He's actually doing butterfly. He's a blur of muscle as he thrashes through the water, his arms cutting through the surface so cleanly that he makes surprisingly little noise.

'That lunatic,' says Lauren, 'is Ned.'

Sadie sits bolt upright, her jaw dropping. Lauren laughs and points at her face.

'That reaction is totally priceless.'

'But—' Sadie says. 'Fucking hell.' So *this* is how you get a swim scholarship to Princeton. Holy shit. The guy's a machine. He's submerged below the surface of the water most of the time, so all she can really see of him are the enormous shoulders and arms that rhythmically power up and out and plough straight down. It's a decent-sized pool, but he's making it look like a paddling pool. By the time he's done his little under-water turn and that funny worm-wiggle that professional swimmers do, he doesn't have much pool length left to do his strokes. She can hardly even spot when he takes his breaths.

It's mesmerising, watching him. Science meets art: the beauty and strength of the male body in action. Plough, plough, plough, turn, and swish. He's in complete harmony with the water. The wingspan of his shoulders and arms, with their rippling, straining muscles, is less like a butterfly and more like a powerful bird of prey. She could watch him all evening. She could watch him every evening. This is so much better than Netflix. But she still can't tell it's Ned, can't equate this anonymous turbo-man with big, shy, dorky Ned. She wonders how long he can keep this up. No breaks, length after length. One thing's for certain: she's not leaving until she sees him get out of that pool.

Lauren breaks her reverie. 'Told you it was worth coming to see him swim, didn't I?'

Sadie turns to her and blinks. 'Can we come every day?'

'I know, right?' Lauren points down the pool. 'And look. We're not the only ones. Those women are eye-fucking him, too.'

It's true. The other two women are both leaning forward, drinks in hand, looking much like Sadie's feeling. A weird and irrational pang of possession hits her. They can fuck off. She takes another slug of wine and wriggles down into her lounger to enjoy the spectacle.

After another few minutes of blissful ogling on their part, Ned comes to a stop at the shallow end of the pool, near their loungers. He stands up and pulls off his goggles, rubbing his eyelids with his thumb and forefinger. She can see now that it really is him. He hasn't spotted them yet. The shallow end has a pretty fan of steps leading out of the pool, and he ascends slowly, shoulders heaving as he catches his breath, allowing Sadie ample opportunity to check him out. He raises an arm to comb his soaking hair off his face.

He's beautiful. So, so beautiful. To think this is what he's been hiding underneath those bulky, baggy work clothes! It's a crime against humanity. He's wearing black Speedos, which would ordinarily be horrifying, but they admirably fulfil their function of leaving as little of his magnificent body to the imagination as is necessary. He's a perfect V; her gaze runs over his swimmer's lats and follows the inward curve down to his hips. There's a smattering of hair on his chest—wet, darkened, curly—that draws her eye down his washboard-flat stomach to where the hair disappears into his trunks. His skin is pale and soaking, the water highlighting the classical lines of his body in the dim light.

The past few days, since the interview, she's been looking at him with new eyes; she's observed him going about his workday. He's serious but never sullen; he's unfailingly professional and polite to everyone who crosses his path. He gets on with things and seeks no praise. There's no ego at play. He can sit at his laptop for hours, focused to a degree that's slightly alarming, but she's also seen how many people at the farm interact with him. The scope of his role boggles her mind.

This act of observing him from whatever seat she's hot-desking at is dangerous. It's dangerous because he's drawing her in, and she has no business being drawn into a man with a girlfriend. She's become aware of him. Her heart lifts when she sees him and falls when he leaves his desk. None of this is good. None of it is healthy or helpful. She needs to keep her head down and her brain free of him, to give him a wide berth.

And now, this. Her feelings have gone from fondness and vague yearning to red fucking hot in an instant. It's as if someone's cranked up a lever inside her. He piqued her interest last week, but last week was the merest tip of the iceberg. Now she's seen the whole package. She can't unsee this. She's opened Pandora's box, gazed into the eyes of Medusa. She's stone. *I need him* screams in her head. She's never had such an instant, visceral reaction to a male body. What would it be like to run her tongue down over those wet biceps, wrap her legs around his cool, soaking skin? It would be inconceivable. Her breathing quickens.

He reaches for a towel that lies a few beds down, and towels his face and hair. Sadie's gaze remains fixed on him, her body frozen, wine glass suspended. He grabs the end of the towel and whips it over one shoulder. A practised, unconscious movement, one he must have done a million times before, but it's so sexy she wants to weep. He looks up, spots them, and freezes for a second, one hand on the towel. Sadie sits up straighter, puts her glass down.

He walks towards them. Their gaze connects, and his eyes narrow as they sweep down the slash of her swimming costume, then back up to her face. He presses his lips together, and the expression on his face makes the heat rise to hers. He's unsmiling. Intense. Something unspoken crackles between them, and her skin tingles. An instant chemical reaction, involuntary and inescapable.

Then he seems to collect himself, and he shoots them a tight smile, a stiff nod, and an awkward *evening*, before he hurries away from them, to the safety of the changing rooms.

Lauren breaks the silence. 'Fuck me, that was hot. Did you see the way he checked you out? You lucky cow.'

'He has a girlfriend.' Sadie is stiff. 'And I've learnt my lesson there.'

'Really? I didn't realise. Good for him. He's such a sweetie; he deserves to be happy. Last year, my nan fell and broke her wrist while I was at work, and Tom was off at some livestock fair with Angus. I was so upset. Ned drove me to the hospital and waited with me until she was discharged, and then he drove us both home. Nan said she'd never met such a nice young man. Isn't that lovely of him?'

As Lauren talks, one thing becomes clear. Nightly visits to this pool are impossible. She can't see him practically naked again. There was no mistaking the heat in his eyes just then when he walked past, but he has a girlfriend, and he's off limits. She'll just have to keep her head down, focus on how bad his diaper-butt chinos and boxy shirts are, and never, ever, allow herself to think about what lies beneath them.

~

NED PRACTICALLY SPRINTS down the corridor to the men's changing rooms. As soon as he's safely through the door, he hits a shower cubicle, peels off his trunks and turns the water on full blast. He's under the deluge before it heats up; the pressure's so high it stings his skin. It's exactly what he needs.

Fuck. Seeing Sadie in her sexy little swimming costume has left him reeling. He wasn't expecting that. He was thinking about her, as ever, as he thrashed out his lengths. He was replaying last week's interview and his brief chat with her on a loop: basking in the weak afterglow of her praise and of the short moments when her eyes reflected something other than disinterest. Swimming and running are the only things that give him any release at present. Focusing on the physical pain, or rather, focusing on trying to blot out the physical pain, is the only salve against the misery and frustration that eat him up.

He saw her dimples four times that day last week. He's clutching at the most meagre straws and it's fucking pathetic. He'd just about wiped her from his mind when he finished up in the pool just now, his mind blessedly blank. Then he clocked her and Lauren, both of them with eyes locked on him.

It's amazing what the brain is capable of when it deems a subject important. Somehow, that fleeting glimpse of her is indelibly printed on his mind's eye. The easy elegance of her body on the lounger. Long, shapely legs. The little black number that looked almost slashed to the navel. The swell of her breasts underneath it. Hair slicked back, as usual. She looked like some Fifties siren—like Grace Kelly, paused in a heavenly snapshot in his mind.

What's really rattled him isn't even seeing her half-naked, but rather the expression on her face and in her eyes as they locked with his. Aside from the brief and welcome respite last week, she's made no secret of her total lack of interest in him, as a colleague and as a guy. But, in that magical bubble of a second, as he walked past and watched her lips part, he could have sworn he saw his own reaction faithfully mirrored in hers: raw desire. It's an image already branded onto his mind's eye, his new favourite image of all time.

LATER THAT NIGHT, Sadie sits on her bed with another glass of wine and her laptop. She should be relaxed after her foot massage and pool-side chill out session, but instead she's a tightly coiled spring. Despite her earlier promise to herself, she can't get Ned out of her head. She mentally flips between a clip of him in full flow in the pool and the heat in his expression when he walked past her in all his glory. Fuck. He's a god, and everything feels upended. Nothing is as she thought it was.

In frustration, she takes a slug from the wineglass on her bedside table. She limited herself to one small glass at the pool before driving home, but she definitely needs and deserves a top-up to take the edge off. She pulls open her laptop and the screen comes to life. She's resisted googling him up until now, but that was before. She's tried to find him on Instagram and Facebook, but to no avail. Now she types in *Ned Fitzsimmons Finance Director Sorrel Farm*, and Google obliges. Nithya asked him something during the interview about his pro bono work; she missed most of what he was saying because she was too busy taking in the way his mouth moved when he talked.

The first worthwhile looking result is his LinkedIn page. She clicks on it, hoping he doesn't have a premium account and can't see who's checking out his profile. If he can, he'll likely assume she's been doing interview prep. She scans it. He's been FD here for over two years; he lists several positions at Deloitte's below that. There are some other live titles too. *Finance Director, Swimming Seals. Coach, Swimming Seals.* A new Google search tells her Swimming Seals is a charity that teaches underprivileged kids to swim and coaches those with the most promise to prepare them for school and university scholarships.

There's a LinkedIn endorsement of several skills from the Swimming Seals founder, a guy called Ben Stevens, and a quote. *Ned Fitzsimmons is one of our most experienced, highly skilled and tireless volunteers, and has secured multiple scholarships for his pupils to independent schools and Russell Group universities. There is no doubt he's changed the course of many children's fortunes while instilling in them a lifelong love of swimming. He also acts as Swimming Seals' pro bono Finance Director. The guy is a total legend.*

She tabs back to the Swimming Seals page and goes to their gallery. There are several shots of Ned in shorts and t-shirt, grinning with groups of children and individuals, all of whom are bedecked with medals and trophies. There's a pain in her heart as she imagines how great he must be with these kids, how kind and patient. He probably loves dorking around with them. His smile in the photos is more open than the ones he hands out at work. He looks gorgeous: relaxed and happy. It's further evidence, if she needed it, of the hidden dimensions she didn't even attempt to see before last week, of his capacity to give of himself.

She changes the Google search: *Ned Fitzsimmons Princeton Swim*. Up comes result after result linking to the *Old Princetonian*'s reportage on the Princeton Tigers. Clicking into them shows records of the swimming and diving team's glory days, with medals and trophies galore. There are also photos: Ned, over a decade younger and in prime sporting shape; narrow in the hips and fucking huge in the shoulders, in tiny speedos. It's wrong to fancy a twenty-year-old, but he looks so beautiful.

The laptop slams shut. She takes another slug of wine and puts the glass down before wriggling back onto her pillow and closing her eyes. She can't help it; she just wants to think about him. It's only been a couple of hours since she saw him; tomorrow is a new day and she'll be a new woman with a will of steel. But tonight doesn't count.

In her mind's eye, she's back at the pool in only her

swimming costume, but this time she and Ned have the fragrant, candlelit orangery to themselves. She reclines on her lounger and watches him as he emerges from the pool, soaking wet. His eyes are fixed on her body as he approaches, that look of unsmiling intensity on his face. He flips his towel over his shoulder in the same way he did earlier and walks towards her, slowly. He leans over her, and droplets of cool water tease her skin. She sinks back into the lounger, paralysed with desire and anticipation, as his gaze roves over her body.

Finally, he kisses her. His tongue is taut in her mouth, and he cups her head in one hand so he can undo the tie at the back of her halter with the other. As he bends his head to suck and tease her nipples in this gripping fantasy, real-life Sadie pulls open her robe and squeezes her own nipples hard, rolling them between her fingers. She groans out loud and her fantasy escalates swiftly: she has no willpower to prolong it. The image of Ned's mouth on her breasts and the reality of her own hands already have her close to the edge.

He peels her swimming costume off and sheds his towel and trunks. He's inside her immediately, and he pins her arms above her head with one hand as he moves inside her. His other hand rubs rhythmically, mercilessly, at the source of her heat, and in the privacy of her bedroom her fingers find the same spot. Definitely no lube needed tonight. She explodes, gasping and bucking, her orgasm dissolving into a bleak awareness that she's alone in this bed and that her own efforts, effective though they were, are no match for the chemical high that would be coursing through her veins right now if she had just come apart in his arms.

18

True to her promise, Sadie sits on her hands all week. If any good has come from this bloody Danny situation, it's that she's a better person than she was. She'd like to think she's gained perspective, empathy. The shock of understanding how far they betrayed his beautiful, pregnant girlfriend is still visceral; it still curdles her stomach. She is not a spoilt child. She cannot just take what she wants and ignore the consequences for others. She will not act in a vacuum. She will not make the same grave moral error of judgement twice. Ned's a test, a hell of a test, and she will not fall at the first fucking hurdle.

But Jesus, does he make it hard. It's like she's been granted unwelcome x-ray vision. Where once she saw a big finance geek dressed like a badly stuffed sausage, now she sees the muscled mass underneath the clothes. Where once he was unmemorable, now his features burn into her consciousness. He's bloody everywhere. Of course, he's always been there. She just hasn't noticed. They share the same office. Everyone hot-desks. Her eyes betray her; they search him out even when her brain's pretending to be otherwise engaged.

All week, she tries to steer clear of him, which is easy enough because he's always in before her. She skulks into work and sits herself as far away as possible from wherever he's set up camp, or over near Lauren, who can always be relied upon for distraction. She sticks close to Evelyn and follows her to any meeting that Evelyn's happy for her to attend. By Friday, she needs a fix of him so badly that she allows herself to sit behind him, one table away. It's close enough that she can hear the muffled, comforting bass of his voice on the phone, but she's purposely limited herself to his back view. If he gets up, she hastily buries her head in her laptop. There's no risk of accidental eye-contact. She drinks in the breadth of his shoulders and the way his hair curls against the nape of his neck. She would give a kidney, right now, to be able to kiss that neck.

On Friday evening, she's in the kitchen area, rehydrating with a pint glass of water. She's heading up to London to hang out with her *Tribune* friends. She's already been to the loos to change and put on her evening makeup. Her dress is seriously short, but it's woolly and clingy, and her thigh-high boots cover most of her legs. Even so, if the guys make her stand outside some shitty pub in this weather, she'll be furious.

A voice behind her says *hey*. Shit. She knows that voice. She swivels. She hasn't planned for this; she's steadfastly avoided any form of contact with him all week.

'Hello,' she manages.

'You look very glamorous.' Ned bends down to retrieve a beer from the glass-fronted fridge next to her, and she clocks his lightening-quick look at her legs before he stands and busies himself with finding a bottle-opener. 'You off out?'

'I'm going out in London.' Her tone is terse and her arms are crossed.

'Fair enough. I suppose Sevenoaks can't quite compete, if you're used to Soho, can it?' He produces his signature smile: shy and gentle.

He's so bloody lovely. He's so fucking *sweet* that she wants to wrap her arms around his neck and her legs around his waist and beg him to take her home with him. But she can't, and if she can't, then she's not going to stand for him making polite, pleasant conversation with her while enjoying the view of her legs. He can fuck off.

'Sevenoaks is a shit-hole,' she tells him. 'Considering everyone around here is supposed to be rich as sin, it's a dump. There's nowhere decent to have a drink, and no one under the age of forty-five.'

He raises his eyebrows. 'I'm sorry we haven't made a good impression on you. But there are some nice places. Maybe a few of us can go out one night—it'd do us good to get away from the farm?'

He's swigging his beer and looking at her in a way that makes her organs turn to syrup and drip down through her torso. She doesn't want a pity drink with him.

'I have no interest in doing that whatsoever.' She pours the rest of her water down the drain and slams the glass into the sink. 'Enjoy your weekend.'

As she flounces off, she catches the hurt disbelief on his face. She fights off the slick of guilt that clings to her. So he thought they were friends, because of a few pleasantries exchanged after the interview the other day. Well, she can't do that. He doesn't get to have a girlfriend at home and be friends with her and enjoy checking out her legs and her swimming costumes. She needs maximum security boundaries here. His hurt feelings are unfortunate collateral damage.

~

GETTING out of Kent was the right thing to do. She stayed with friends on Friday night and begrudgingly caught the train back down to Sevenoaks on Saturday. Leaving Charing Cross felt like a death sentence. She loves Sorrel Farm so much, but the rest of Kent seems overrated. Maybe she can beg a cottage on the farm. The thought of the cottages reminds her of Danny, and she shudders.

After a dry evening with Netflix on Saturday, she feels more human on Sunday, and perspective seeps slowly back through her veins. She gives herself a pep talk. She will be fine. She has a job she loves, and a huge opportunity to make a name for the farm. She believes in the management team and in the company's vision. She has friends—Evelyn, Jess and Lauren, at least. She's a big girl. She'll settle into Sevenoaks and she'll save as aggressively as possible so she can find a place that feels more like home.

She buys herself a bacon roll and a cup of tea on the high street and polishes the former off quickly. It's Remembrance Sunday, and it's almost eleven o'clock: nearly time for the two minutes' silence. She's always appreciated the solemnity of this occasion, the chance for communities to unite and meditate on the unimaginable sacrifices ordinary people made decades ago so they can go about their lives today, blithely unaware of how remarkable it is that life is unremarkable now. Usually she tunes in on TV and enjoys the stirring, haunting chords of Elgar's *Nimrod* over footage of the Cenotaph in London.

Today, though, she hovers on the edge of a large crowd of people at the war memorial in the centre of Sevenoaks, sipping her tea and bowing her face to her cup to warm it. As she waits for the period of silence to begin, she looks to her left and freezes. Ned is a few metres away, wrapped up in a long, black coat and scarf. In front of him stands a beautiful, slender girl, also in black. He has his arm hooked around her collarbones, pulling her to him, and his chin rests on the top of her head. There's a poppy pinned to her lapel, and her long, dark hair spills over his coat sleeve. Both their faces are pale and taut. He puts his other arm around her. Sadie flees.

The shock of actually seeing him with her is sickening. It means she's real, and he's indisputably in a relationship. Outside of the work bubble that frames the context for her interactions with him, he has a life with a beautiful girlfriend who finds refuge in his arms. It's the slap in the face she needs, the sanity check that reminds her to ignore the looks he's been giving her and do the right thing: leave him and this poor girl to their relationship.

~

AFTER THE TWO-MINUTE SILENCE ENDS, Caroline turns around and buries her face in Ned's chest.

'Thanks for coming with me.' Her voice is muffled.

'Of course.' He hugs her. 'I want to pay my respects as much as you do. And I'd never let you come alone.'

'Sometimes it gets to me,' she says. 'So much fucking sacrifice and misery, century after century. It feels like we're running to stand still.'

'I know.' He releases her and links his arm through hers. 'Let's get you a coffee.'

'Have you heard from him recently?' She looks up at him.

'We exchanged quick emails last week. You?'

'He Skyped me yesterday. God, I miss him so much. It's so much worse on the weekends. Thanks for babysitting me—above and beyond, as ever.'

'I can only imagine. And you never need to thank me. You're part of the family, and one day he'll make an honest woman of you. Till then, as long as he's away, I'm here for you. I promised my baby brother I'd look after his girl, and I meant it. You're not alone, Caz.'

It's a shitty situation for her, but she's a trooper. Jimmy has been in the army for as long as he and Caroline have been dating, which must be eleven or twelve years. They met in sixth form college. She's now as much of an army wife as the rest of them, even if she doesn't have the ring to prove it yet. Jimmy's a lucky man to have her.

When they've got their coffees, she turns to him. 'Any gossip?'

He grins. 'You're unfailingly optimistic, I'll give you that.'

'What about that girl at work? You still pining?'

'Sadie. Yes, I'm still pining. And yes, she's still ignoring me. She thawed out briefly last week, or so I thought, but she bit my head off the other day when I suggested socialising after work, so...'

He shrugs his shoulders. He really hoped the FT interview would be the start of a more cordial relationship with her, even if she wasn't ready to head off into the sunset with him just yet. But her outright hostility on Friday stunned him. He'd approached her with hope—and not a small amount of lust, especially given those boots she was wearing. But she was prickly beyond belief. She couldn't have made her disinterest any clearer.

'What the fuck is her problem?' Caroline looks as if she wants to exhale fire. 'She could never do any better than you. She needs a good slap. You're the real deal, Ned.'

'Tell that to Princess Charmless.' He sighs. 'I'm punching way above my weight. I saw her by the pool the other night. She had this unbelievable black swimming costume on that was slashed all the way down here.' He indicates. 'She looked so hot, I nearly exploded, right there by the pool. I had to make a run for it to the showers.'

'Ew.' She makes a face. 'That is far too much information. You're like my brother, for God's sake. I just don't want to think about you shooting your load over some girl. If she doesn't come to her senses soon, you need to move on.'

19

Seeing Ned with his girlfriend has proven to be the catalyst Sadie needed to pull her finger out and focus on work. And she does. She's been pulling more weight since Danny-gate, but Ned's distracted her over the past few weeks, and that's not on. There's only one person she should focus on and that's Evelyn. Whatever Evelyn wants, Sadie will get for her.

She expands her spreadsheet of press contacts to include more overseas journalists and influencers. She goes heavy on the US. Sorrel Farm is catnip for American visitors. Several US-based influencers flew in for the party announcing Evelyn's investment this summer, and they fell hard for the place. Attracting more guests like this will be key. She gets out and about, meeting London-based targets in person as much as she can. It gives her space from the office, and being in London is always energising.

She's also helping Evelyn to contact British brands with whom they can work. This is the fun bit, where PR and business development coincide. Evelyn has secured the designer Astrid Carmichael to sponsor the Sorrel Farm Christmas event, and they spend a wildly exciting afternoon with Astrid at the farm, finalising the logistics. Also present is Siobhan Quinn, the famous event planner who worked such magic on the summer party.

There's a moment in the meeting where Sadie feels completely happy with her lot. She's sitting in the Oast House with Evelyn, whom she adores, Astrid, a platinum blonde beauty who's as warm as she is elegant, and Siobhan, from whose scarlet mouth pours an unending stream of creativity. There's a synergy, a flow, between these women, and she can't recall the last time she felt so creatively stimulated. They discuss how wonderful the effect—and scent—of eucalyptus swags, garlands and wreaths will be. They debate the relative merits of dotting the poser tables with taper candles in tall glass sleeves or tiny brass lamps with pleated silk shades. One of Astrid's signature prints for the season, featuring swirling trails of ivy, will be used for the table linen. They're not solving world hunger, but it's a vivacious and creatively fulfilling conversation between four smart women, and it reminds Sadie that if she wants to keep her head free of men (one man in particular), she must fill it with the company of stimulating women more often.

To that end, she hustles Valerie Drax to agree to have lunch with her. She very much enjoyed the older woman's company at the Harvest Festival and besides, she needs to pin her down regarding Zoe's feature in the magazine. They've chatted a bit on email over the past month, but Valerie's been elusive. Time for a charm offensive.

They meet at The Wolseley on Piccadilly. It's Valerie's choice, but it so perfectly epitomises everything Sadie misses about London that she could cry. The day is revoltingly wet and the pavements are slick with rain, but once she's settled inside the Wolseley's marbled monochrome splendour, all feels right with the world. She feels like herself. Her Proenza Schouler trousers, bought at a sample sale and still the most expensive item she's ever owned, fit in here. Not like at Sorrel Farm, where no one except Evelyn would have the faintest clue what Proenza is.

Valerie isn't one to beat about the bush.

'I've been pitching hard to my editor. He's interested. We're thinking late Jan, early Feb. Deep winter. People are in full hibernation then; we go heavy on the seasonal recipes in those months.'

'That's fantastic news.' Sadie begins to speak, but Valerie cuts her off with a hand up before taking a swig of her red wine.

'I think—*think*, mind you—I can even get you a cover. But the food alone won't cut it. We'd need Zoe, to draw the readers in. We can do a feature on her followed by a selection of recipes: three or four. The feature needs to focus on her approach to food; big themes if she wants; points of difference. But not preachy. It should be immersive. Everyone's bored shitless at that time of year. Let's give them something to get excited about. She's fucking gorgeous; it'll be a little escapism for everyone. I know I'd like to hibernate in Sorrel Farm for the whole of winter and have Zoe cook for me; let's conjure up that vibe for our readers.'

This is amazing. Evelyn will be ecstatic. Zoe will hate it, but this is the route Evelyn is intent on going down. Sadie suspects Zoe won't have a choice.

That afternoon, they do a little hibernating of their own. Over creamed potatoes and excellent *coq au vin* washed down with more red wine, they put the world to rights.

'I have to ask.' Valerie puts down her fork and folds her arms on the table. 'What happened with that hot guy? Did you get it on after Nigel and I left you to it?'

Sadie has been hoping she won't ask, but that's a futile exercise where an experienced hack like Valerie is concerned. She's not the type to let a good story evade her. She groans.

'Oh, God. It was a fucking nightmare.'

'No! How so? You were getting on famously when we left.'

'This is between us, ok?' She takes a deep breath. 'I did sleep with him that night. He'd managed to get a room at the farm—jammy bastard that he is—because he was on the early shift the next morning. So I went back with him. And —it was great.'

'Okay…? So what's the problem?'

Sadie squirms. It's still excruciating to revisit the episode out loud—or in her own head, for that matter.

'A few days later, his devoted girlfriend popped up in the office. He'd forgotten his lunch.'

She pauses and looks up at Valerie, who winces.

'Ouch.'

'It gets worse. She's pregnant.'

'Christ.' Valerie's face pinches in distaste. 'What an utter cock.'

'I know.' Sadie rubs her face in her hands. 'I confronted him, obviously. He said she was having a really tough pregnancy, and basically he wasn't getting any action. So he came after me.'

'Oh, for fuck's sake. How pathetic. And poor you.' Valerie leans across and pats Sadie's hand. 'But I hope you haven't been beating yourself up about this.'

'Well,' Sadie says softly. 'I'm not sure I'm entirely blameless.'

'How so?'

'There were whispers that he had a girlfriend.' She shifts

uncomfortably. 'I had no idea it was serious, or that she was pregnant, of course. But to be honest, I didn't want to know. I thought about asking him right before I sloped off to that hotel room with him, but I had my eye on the prize and I didn't want anything sabotaging it.'

'Listen to me.' Valerie's expression is firm. 'This is not on you. This is *all* on him. He's a grown man—he's going to be a father, for fuck's sake—and he should be capable of doing right by his partner and not betraying her when she needs him most. That's nothing to do with you.'

Sadie washes down her mouthful of chicken with a swig of wine. 'I'd like to believe you, but I'm not sure. It seems to be my MO: trampling all over people to get what I want.'

'Men have trampled all over people to get what they want for centuries, darling. It's called ambition, and it shouldn't be a dirty word for you just because you don't have a penis. It's not your responsibility to ensure other people behave themselves: that's plain exhausting. Focus on working hard and being transparent and fair, and you should be able to look yourself in the mirror quite happily.'

'That's what I'm trying to do now,' Sadie admits. 'Keep my head down, hustle, and don't get carried away by my own press. I'm here to do a job for a wonderful team of people; that's my top priority.'

'Quite right. Sorrel Farm is a very special cause to promote. And you'll do a wonderful job for them. Let's see if we can't swing you a *Sunday Times Magazine* cover feature to get you on your way, eh?'

The older woman's kindness makes Sadie feel uncharacteristically emotional. It must show, for Valerie tuts.

'Now, now. Buck up. I'm not doing this as a favour; I'm doing it because I know Zoe's face will sell newspapers and her philosophy will resonate with our readers.' As she tops up both their glasses, she adds:

'And don't forget to have some fun along the way. You're allowed to, you know? Including finding yourself a guy, if you want to—ideally someone who's not a total dipshit. Is there anyone?'

Ned's face swims before her eyes: a face so sweet and kind and handsome that she still can't believe she didn't value it when she had the chance.

'There is someone—also at work, unfortunately. And he's everything Danny isn't, believe me. He's so thoughtful, and he has bucket loads of integrity. But I missed my chance with him. He definitely has a girlfriend now—I saw them together a couple of weeks ago. And I've learnt my lesson there. So that's that.'

'I'm sorry to hear that,' Valerie says. 'He sounds far more deserving of you. But do me a favour, darling. Please don't let any feelings of unworthiness fester and sabotage your chance of happiness. Next time you find someone you're interested in, know that you are allowed to be happy with them.'

The pep talk serves to slacken the band of guilt that has sat tightly around her chest for the past few weeks, but it does nothing to dull the ache of longing for Ned. It's too hard to get over him. She's stuck to her promise not to think too much about what lies under his clothes. Luckily, he makes this easier for her by continuing to hide his physique under the same revolting work attire.

But harder to ignore is the essence of *him* with all its facets that make him so fascinating to her, mainly the fact that his intellect coexists so seamlessly with an utter absence of ego. He's the most humble person in the office and yet, whenever he opens his mouth in a meeting or huddle or in her presence, his authority is indisputable and his mastery of numbers is jaw-dropping. He has everything: implacable self-assurance that's hot as hell, and a *niceness* that she would never, ever have expected to find attractive and which has somehow become the single most irresistible thing about him. No matter. He's not hers. Lucky, lucky girlfriend.

20

On the morning of the last Monday in November, Sadie heads straight for the table in the office where the day's papers are laid out. She grabs the *FT* and puts her bag and laptop down on a quiet corner of one of the tables. Her morning cup of tea can wait. Spreading out the broadsheet in front of her, she leafs impatiently through the pages. There it is. Ned's *FT on FDs* column. In her former life, she never got tired of seeing her byline in print, and it's equally gratifying in this job to see the Sorrel Farm articles she's brought about pop up. As she gets into her stride, the frequency of these articles is increasing. But this is different. Today is Ned's big day.

She scans the column. It's set up as a straightforward Q&A under Nithya's byline, and it's a faithful representation of what she and Ned discussed last month. The photo of his beautiful face is inevitably compromised by the graininess of the print edition, but the essence of him sings out from the page, both from his image and his words. She's continued to avoid him like the plague since seeing him at the Cenotaph and discussing him at the lunch with Valerie, but not today. She can't wait to show him. It's a momentous occasion for him. Her mind flicks unhelpfully back to those old online news reports in the *Daily Princetonian*; she mentally slaps them down.

She folds the paper so the column is facing outwards, and hurries around to where he's already sitting, a couple of tables away, hunched over his laptop with his AirPods in. She takes a brief moment to enjoy the view of his profile before he spots her. He has a pen to his mouth, and he taps it against his lower lip. Lucky pen. When she gets close enough for him to sense her presence, he looks up and flinches. It's upsetting, but not surprising. She's been such a nasty little bitch to him that she can't blame him for reacting with fear.

His natural good manners take over and he pulls his AirPods out.

'Hi.' He's cautious, eyes darting, presumably trying to work out why she's bothering him. Since her rudeness to him in the kitchen that evening, he's made no voluntary contact with her. It's hurtful and miserable, but she knows it's for the best.

She gives him a dazzling smile. 'Today's the day.' She throws the paper onto the table next to his laptop, his column clearly visible. She watches his expression change as he clocks it.

'Oh, wow.' He raises his face to her, an instinctive grin of wonder that he can't wipe off. 'That's pretty cool. I had no idea they were running it today.'

She's still smiling at him. She can't help it. It's stupid, but she's so irrationally thrilled that she's been able to do one thing to make him happy, to put that gorgeous grin on his face.

'It looks great.' She gestures at the paper. 'You come across really well. Have a read. And congratulations.'

She nods, and spins on her heel as he thanks her.

On paper, it's a good day. Just before their regular Monday management meeting, she receives a WhatsApp from Valerie Drax, telling they have a firm date for Zoe's feature: Sunday 27th January 2019. When she shares the news at the meeting, everyone is ecstatic. Evelyn and Jess are so excited they can barely contain themselves. Zoe smiles her serene smile and says some lovely words of thanks. Ned, seemingly mellowed by their successful interaction earlier, tells her in enthusiastic terms what an amazing job she's done and how big a step the feature will be towards putting the farm on the map.

She allows herself a minute to bask in the warmth and kindness of these lovely people, and to acknowledge to herself that she's done what she set out to do, what Evelyn told her was her biggest goal for the season. She's achieved it. It will be another milestone for this wonderful community, and it's mainly her doing. In that moment, she feels the glow of acceptance and belonging. But as she looks across the table at the incredible man grinning at her, her heart is breaking. This moment is fleeting, and it's grounded in a professional win, nothing more. This is as good as it gets with him.

21

Once they get their date for the interview, everything moves quickly. Since Evelyn had her heart-to-heart with Zoe, their communication around the book has been far more open and healthy. Zoe's a new woman, the weight of the world seemingly lifted from her shoulders, and she's even allowed herself to get excited about the book. It shows; she and Clara have been working tirelessly on making, styling and shooting her favourite seasonal recipes. The result is a collection of gorgeous shots, from fly-on-the-wall footage of Zoe and her team cooking to mouth-watering plated creations.

Autumn is a wonderful time for puddings, and the air in the Oast House kitchen is heavy with aromas of sugar and spice as Zoe poaches fruits, makes syrups and jams, and simmers compotes. Pickling is a serious business at Sorrel Farm, too, both as a way to preserve the seasonal bounty for the barren winter months and to minimise wastage.

One of Zoe's team, a Polish chef called Lena, is the pickling quartermaster. The result is endless large glass jars of ferment, utilising scraps from the Walled Garden, as well as jars of whole pickled lemons, carrots, onions, peppers, and whatever else Lena can commandeer to capture in glass. The jewel-like colours of the pickles are a wonderful symbol of the abundance of the farm's produce, and Clara goes mad for them. It's likely that the art of pickling will earn its own chapter in Zoe's book.

It's wonderful to see Zoe allow herself to be creatively unleashed in this project, and it's gratifying for all of them to have found a way to immortalise her creations, whose fleeting existence usually ends when met with an appreciative customer. The day before Valerie Drax is due to descend on the farm for the interview, Evelyn loiters in the kitchen. She's heard panna cotta's on the menu today, and she's damned if she's going to miss that. Zoe hands her a plate. On it is a flawless, milky panna cotta with compote Zoe made last month from the last of the blackberries, and a scattering of toasted hazelnuts. Evelyn's mouth waters.

'You angel.' She grabs a spoon and kisses Zoe. 'This looks sublime.'

Zoe picks up her mug and gestures. 'I'm due a break. I'll come and sit with you while you eat.'

They make their way over to a small table by the window, flanked with little velvet armchairs.

'So.' Evelyn lowers herself into her chair. 'You nervous about tomorrow?'

Zoe shrugs. 'A little, I suppose.'

'Not getting cold feet?'

'No! I wouldn't do that to you and Sadie, not after all her hard work.'

'Glad to hear it.' Evelyn takes a spoonful of panna cotta. It's heaven: the aromatic silkiness of the *cooked cream* is the perfect offset for the brittle, toasted nuts and the sweet-sour richness of the blackberries. 'Oh my God,' she sighs. 'This is amazing.'

'It's good to see you eating,' Zoe comments. 'When you first came, you wouldn't let dairy pass your lips. Angus is a good influence.'

'And you're a bad influence. But you're right; Sadie's done a phenomenal job, pulling this off so quickly. I'm impressed. She's really off to a flying start.'

'I like her a lot,' Zoe says thoughtfully. 'No bullshit.'

'That's what I like, too.' Evelyn swallows another dreamy mouthful. 'And she really gets things done. She's motoring along with building a great list of press contacts. She's brutally efficient. I'm just worried she's not very happy.'

'Does she not enjoy the job?' Zoe asks.

'She does, I think—very much. But she's lonely. She's a city girl; I'm not sure she should be languishing in Sevenoaks. I'm worried it was too big a move for her.'

'Then we must include her more.' Zoe's tone is firm. 'We're a family here. She's your right-hand woman; we can't have her being lonely and unhappy. We'll be around her, making sure she is okay. It's no hardship. Jess really likes her too.'

Evelyn reaches over and squeezes her hand. 'Thank you, sweetie. You're right. I've been so distracted by… everything. I need to take her under my wing more, outside of work. She's a keeper; we need her to be happy. Now, do you want to talk any more about the interview before I inhale the rest of this and head back to the office?'

'One thing,' Zoe says. 'I've been thinking a lot about my past since our conversation, and I feel things shifting for me. I wonder if it's time to start talking about it. Not, you know, to make a big deal of it, but to be open about what happened to me. I don't feel the need to inflict my thoughts on the afterlife on everybody, but if my experience is the starting point for the way I view the world, and farming, and how we use food to commune with nature, then perhaps it should be part of the conversation.'

Evelyn puts down her spoon. She hasn't been expecting this turnaround, but it's a welcome one, and it makes sense. She doesn't want to exploit Zoe's backstory, but here is a unique soul with a unique way of viewing the world, and if they tread carefully, Zoe's experiences can add depth and authenticity to her food philosophy.

'I think that makes a lot of sense,' she tells Zoe now. She looks at her watch. 'I need Sadie to get hold of Valerie and let her know we've expanded the remit for the interview.'

~

THANKS TO EVELYN'S HEADS-UP, Sadie knows something's afoot, but she has no idea what else Zoe plans to discuss with Valerie. She faces the interview with a fair amount of trepidation. This is the biggest coup of her career: the *Sunday Times Magazine*'s circulation is multiples of the *Tribune*'s Sunday supplement. It's unnerving and unhelpful to think Zoe may have a curveball to throw at them, but she trusts Evelyn, and Evelyn trusts Zoe, so she has no choice but to go along for the ride. At least her cryptic message to Valerie has piqued the journalist's interests.

Zoe has elected to hold the interview at her farmhouse, away from the bustle of the kitchen. Sadie hasn't been there before, and she's stunned by the beauty of the glass box they find themselves sitting in, around a beautiful old oak table whose surface is worn to a satiny sheen. The room has one-eighty degree views of the farmhouse's lawns, stretching all the way to the ancient wall and concealed door that must surely lead through the walled garden on one side. The trees in the garden are almost bare and they stand like ballerinas between the house and the stubbled fields beyond. She feels her heart rate dropping just by virtue of being here.

Valerie has allowed Sadie and Evelyn to stay for the interview. Evelyn wants to be around to prompt Zoe to follow certain angles which will lay the foundations for marketing the book next year. She's told Sadie that she's planning on getting back in touch with Avery from Penguin after this interview, with an exciting, additional angle for the book and to tell her Zoe has agreed to be the face of the book. What this exciting angle is, or what's driven Zoe's about-face, Sadie can't wait to find out.

Once the recorder's running, Valerie plunges straight in. 'Zoe, Evelyn tells me you have another angle you'd like to propose we consider in the remit of this conversation—something about your past? Can you tell me a bit more about it, then we'll decide which way to go with this?'

Sadie watches Zoe curiously. She's in a deep red woollen dress today, and she's glowing as usual. She also looks strangely calm.

'Yes, it's about my past. I haven't spoken about this before; even Evelyn didn't know about it until a couple of months ago, and I've known her for years. But it has a bearing on how I live my life, and on my relationship with nature, and with food, so I'd like to talk about it now.'

Valerie smiles. 'I'm all ears.' It's a smile of encouragement, but it's also a smile that says *I feel a story coming on.* Sadie remembers that feeling.

'When I was twelve, I had an operation to remove a brain tumour,' Zoe says matter-of-factly. 'It was unsuccessful, and I died on the table. According to the surgical team, I was clinically dead for six minutes. They had abandoned resuscitation efforts and pronounced me dead, when my heart and brain functions restarted. Within weeks, my tumour had vanished all by itself.'

She pauses. Sadie's jaw feels slack as she computes what she's hearing. Valerie looks exactly the same. Zoe seems to be doing Valerie the courtesy of pausing to see if she has a question, but none are forthcoming. She's speechless.

Zoe continues. 'This is not the place for a discussion about the existence of consciousness beyond this physical life, and I don't want to inflict my views on your readers. But I do know what I saw, and what I understood during the period that I was dead. I was shown that all life on this planet, human or animal or plant, is interwoven in the most beautiful way, in a web so intricate and perfect that it's impossible to comprehend.

'Meeting Jess years later, and taking on the management of Sorrel Farm with her, was the starting point of my journey to make peace with the insights I'd received. Before that, I struggled to live with them. Years of therapy and a theology degree had failed to bring me peace. Training to be a chef in France was wonderful, but it lacked the purpose that I felt I should be searching for. But here, I can see how everything should be, and our amazing team is gradually restoring this slice of nature on the farm to its rightful equilibrium. We're communing with nature, and as we commune, we learn. And eating in a way that is respectful, and seasonal, and gives back as much as it takes, is the food philosophy my team and I espouse here. I truly believe that one of the ways we can all experience this heaven on earth, or the interconnectedness of the universe, is to eat this way.'

It's clear from the questions that follow, as Valerie rallies and her journalistic instinct guides her, that this story is far bigger than the one they initially promised her. If Sadie had to guess, she'd say Valerie doesn't have much time for anything that may be perceived as woo-woo. But she knows authenticity when she sees it, and her engagement with Zoe and her story tells Sadie she intends to weave a full picture of Zoe, including this staggering backstory that's informed her current vocation, for the *Sunday Times* readers.

Sadie, meanwhile, is reeling. She stares openly at Zoe during the rest of the interview. This is the reason for her weirdness during that first meeting with Penguin. As Zoe spins a true story more fantastical than any fairytale, Sadie has goosebumps under her thick sweater. Zoe seems more angelic than human, which now makes sense. She elevates everything she touches and describes. The way she describes the delights of nurturing ourselves with the best of what nature has to offer, in a way that suits our human needs each season, makes total sense. How the earth soaks up fallen autumnal leaves to sustain its life during the dead, winter months, is suddenly a perfect analogy for how we can sustain ourselves through winter with nourishment from our plates. It will be just the piece to inspire and educate in deepest winter. Sadie feels galvanised just from having been present. The importance of what the team here is trying to achieve is brought newly home. And she has a part to play in putting them on the map.

When Valerie takes her leave, she's her usual, warmly brusque, self.

'They don't make many like her,' she tells Sadie as she kisses her on both cheeks. 'I already know the title for this. I'll call it *Heaven on Earth.*'

22

As soon as Evelyn puts her key in the lock and pushes open the heavy front door, she's aware of a difference in the atmosphere that she can't put her finger on. The hallway is warm and scented with heavenly pine and eucalyptus, thanks to the fresh garland winding its way down the entirety of Belvedere's sweeping banister. She peers through the large archway into the main drawing room. The fire crackles behind the grate, and the enormous Christmas tree they decorated last weekend stands proudly in the window, lights twinkling softly. Eddie's not here: he's seeing the panto at the London Palladium this weekend with Seb and Gino, and Seb picked him up from school a couple of hours ago.

'Maria?' she calls. 'Angus?'

His voice calls from the back of the house. 'In the garden room. Come through.'

She slips off her coat and stashes her stuff on a chair before heading towards Angus' voice. Christmas choral music floats through the air, and she catches the smell of something incredible cooking in the kitchen. What *is* that?

What is Angus up to? She turns the corner, and the scene that faces her makes her stop dead. Her hand flies to her mouth, goosebumps erupt all over her skin, and a huge wave of emotion rises up her body as understanding hits her.

They haven't decorated the garden room, but now it's transformed. She takes in the dozens of candles whose flickering lights are reflected a hundred-fold: it's pitch black outside, and the glass-sided room is a giant mirror. Mounds of velvety, dark red roses stand on every surface. Gold baubles dangle from the chandelier and reflect the candlelight back around the room like little disco balls. There are swags of fresh greenery everywhere. The effect is spellbinding, but the decorations aren't what's causing this wave of emotion inside her. No, that's coming from the man who stands in the centre of the room, waiting for her, his face so full of love and hope and nerves that it's impossible to misinterpret his intention.

'Hi, sweetheart.' He steps forward and holds his hands out to her, and she walks into his arms in a daze. He wraps himself around her and kisses her head before releasing her.

'You've probably clocked what's going on here.' There's a tremor in his voice that almost breaks her heart. 'So I won't string this out.' He cups her face in his hands and his eyes crinkle in the warm, loving way that she adores as he gazes at her. 'I love you so much, sweetheart. I can't live without you; I don't want any life you're not a part of. Will you do me the honour of being my wife?'

Her eyes are wet, even as her smile threatens to crack her face in two. The rush of blood to her head is giving her an out-of-body experience. 'Yes, please. *Yes.*' She kisses him, hard. 'Try and stop me.'

He manages a quick *phew* before he kisses her back, and they melt together for a few moments. She can feel relief, and total commitment, and endless passion in his kiss. As she winds her arms around him as tightly as they'll go, she thinks, *this is my* husband. *I'll wake up next to him for the rest of our lives. Thank God.* The delicious warmth of his body, its length pressed against hers, radiates into her.

He pulls his face away. 'We'll choose a ring together. I suspected you'd have some strong views. And it's no mean feat, trying to match that robin's egg you were wearing when I met you.'

She laughs. 'I don't want another rock like that. It's not appropriate for a farmer's wife. Maybe something more modest.'

'There's nothing modest about your taste in diamonds.' He kisses her nose. 'But we'll find something worthy of you. We can go into town next week and make a day of it.'

She winds her arms around his shoulders and sighs indulgently. He smiles at her.

'That's a big sigh.'

'It's a good sigh. I'm so happy. I wasn't expecting this yet. You're a fast worker, aren't you? The ink is barely dry on the divorce papers.'

'You've been back on the market for two weeks. That's two weeks too long for my liking.'

'This isn't one of your livestock markets, darling. I'm not a prize heifer.'

'You're my prize heifer and'—his hands slide down over her bum and squeeze it—'that's a fine rump you've got there.'

'I hadn't realised you were going to turn into a chauvinist the moment I agreed to marry you. And I was never on the market. I was always, always yours.'

He kisses her again, a slow, soft kiss that melts her bones. She's drunk on him, just as she always is when he pulls this move. A lifetime of this she can definitely do.

'Don't worry, sweetheart.' His voice is a caress in her ear. 'I'm under no illusions about who wears the trousers in this relationship. I wouldn't have it any other way. And I'm not taking this as a firm yes until you've had a chance to talk to Eddie. I know this is a huge deal for both of you.'

It's just like him to say something like that. He's already proven his commitment to Eddie a million times over.

'I think we know which way he'll go.' She leads him over to the sofa. 'You've been running a dirty campaign there—it stinks of bribery.'

'I've been lobbying him shamelessly,' he agrees. 'Haribo and tractor rides go a long way. Seriously, though, I'll never try to replace Seb, but I love Eddie and I want to make a long-term commitment to both of you. He's an amazing little guy.'

~

Some time later, they lie back down on the sofa after eating mouth-watering venison from Angus' family estate in Derbyshire. She didn't clock it when she walked into the room, but a beautifully set table for two sat in the corner. Angus confessed over dinner that he'd enlisted the help of Siobhan Quinn, Evelyn's favourite event planner, to deck the garden room out for the proposal. Siobhan spent the day here, working her festive magic.

'My mind is racing,' she confesses. 'We have a whole life to plan—it's so exciting!'

'I'm thinking world domination, if you are?' His fingers

trace a lazy line up and down the front of her sweater, making her shiver.

'I'll leave world domination to Seb, I think. I'm getting too old for that kind of thing. And you're definitely too old.'

'Charming.' His hand moves down over her thigh.

'I'll settle for success right here, in our corner of the world,' she says thoughtfully. 'A happy family life, building this charity together, and of course, lots of growth for Sorrel Farm. Don't worry, my ambitions are as lofty as ever where the farm is concerned.'

'I wouldn't expect anything less. But I did have an idea for another... project that it may be fun to work on together. I'd enjoy the process, at least.'

'What's that?'

He pulls away just enough for her to focus on his face properly. 'Well...' He seems to be choosing his words carefully. 'It's something you alluded to when we were in France: your regret that you never got to have a baby brother or sister for Eddie. I know you've got a lot on your plate, but if you'd like to try for a baby, it's something I'd be very much on board with.'

This is even more of a shock than the proposal. She struggles to sit up, her mind reeling. He's offering her a lifetime together, and another baby—something she never thought she'd have. This man is too much. She puts her hand up to his face and strokes his stubbly cheek.

'I had no idea you felt this way.' Her eyes search his and find his reply in his steadfast gaze. 'Really? You'd be up for going through all that again? I feel like you're so far out of it...'

'So far, I must have amnesia,' he tells her. 'I've forgotten how the sleepless nights feel and how bad the nappies smell. All I can think of is that if we made a baby together, he or she would be the most adored baby in the world. And we'd have a village to help raise them.'

'It would definitely be a case of bringing your baby to work, wouldn't it? God, I don't know.'

'We don't need to decide just yet. It's a huge decision, but I never want you to regret not having had another kid; it's far too big a regret to live with and it's just not necessary. We can keep the stabilisers on for now. But we can practice practicing, if you get my drift.'

She loves him so much, she might die from it. She thought she was happy before, but in one evening he's offered her all she's ever wanted, on a platter. *Her husband.* The future is sweet and bright, and filled with love and hope. He's watching her face, waiting for her answer.

'I think doing a pre-practice practice is an excellent idea,' she says. 'Just to, you know, refine our technique. Let's go consummate this engagement.'

23

By the time the Midwinter party comes around, Sadie feels as though she's limping to the finish line. The preparations have consumed her and Evelyn throughout December, and for that distraction she's very grateful. Next week is Christmas, and all she can think about is getting herself back to her parents' house in Ealing and spending a few days in bed with a bottle of wine and a tin of Quality Streets. She couldn't be more of a Bridget Jones cliché if she tried.

She's been taking her vitamins and staying off the booze as much as is possible during the festive period. Even so, she feels the weariness in her bones and she knows what's causing it. Her love of her job keeps her professional mojo alive, and she throws herself into chasing up journos and influencers, hustling them to confirm their attendance and cajoling them to promise prominent features and footage on their platforms. There's also plenty of communication with Astrid Carmichael's team, who'll be dressing Evelyn and some of the higher profile influencers for the event.

Any fly on the wall during office hours would conclude

that Sadie Thomas is on fire, but in the evenings, when she collapses in her bedroom, she's a different person. She feels like a shadow, gloomy and insubstantial. She can't even treat herself to the heavenly warmth of the orangery pool, in case she comes face to face with Ned in all his glory. In the office, he's a machine. He works and works and works. He's always there when Sadie arrives in the morning, and he's still there when she leaves, albeit with a bottle of beer by his laptop. She has the uncharitable thought that his girlfriend can't be doing her job properly if he spends so much time at work and so little time smiling. If she was his girlfriend, he'd be in late every morning and his grin would be face-splitting; she'd make sure of it.

The day of the party is crazy with last-minute preparations, and she can't help but get swept up in the festive atmosphere. The office crackles with excitement, but amazingly, no one seems overly stressed. Siobhan Quinn manages her events team with the precision of a world-class conductor. Most of the office staff are attending, as the format is informal: a carol service and stalls around huge fire pits in the walled garden, before mounds of bowl food and vats of alcohol back in the Oast House, where they'll have a big knees-up.

Sadie was finding it hard to decide what to wear until a wildly exciting conversation a few days ago with Diana, her equivalent at Astrid Carmichael.

'Astrid suggested you should wear something from the brand,' Diana said on the phone. 'She thinks you're gorgeous, and since you'll be the point-person for the press at your end, it makes sense that you wear Astrid.'

Sadie didn't need to be asked twice. It wasn't likely she'd have a chance to wear such a luxurious brand on her own ticket any time soon. Consequently, tonight she finds herself in a short, strappy gold lamé dress that's necessitated an emergency spray-tan, and a huge black faux-fur coat. Both are incredible, but as she hobbles over the freezing cobblestones of the courtyard in delicate gold sandals, she curses the fact that she's not wearing winter boots. The balls of her feet are absolute agony; she's not sure how she's going to last the evening.

In the event, she acquits herself well. She can't help but be transported by the wonderful festivities in the walled garden, whose illuminated fruit trees bewitch the guests. Choristers from a local all-boys boarding school sing on a dais, the purity of their notes reaching far and wide over the throng of voices. She finds herself having fun, the free-flowing *vin chaud* warming her from the inside out and loosening her tension. She gossips with Nigel and Valerie in between flitting to flatter and attend to the various influencers who are there. Most are in reveries over the abundance of social media opportunities here. Siobhan has surpassed herself; the garden is an Instagrammer's dream. Servers dressed as nutcrackers hand out oxtail soup and sausage rolls, and burlap-festooned stalls at the edges of the garden offer all manner of free delicacies, from very British mince pies to German stollen.

She's on her way to find Diana and check that Astrid is happy with the way the evening is unfolding, when the guests ahead of her clear and she comes face to face with Ned. He's with that girl again, both wrapped up warmly. Their noses and cheeks are rosy and they're laughing. He holds both their paper cups while she wipes trails of what looks like *vin chaud* off the furry lapel of her coat with a napkin. Sadie freezes, and Ned starts, but he's clearly in too good a mood to be bothered by her.

'Hi Sadie.' His tone is cheerful. 'Meet Caroline.'

'Nice to meet you.' Caroline waves the hand clutching the napkin and continues giggling. 'I'm such an idiot. Excuse me.'

She resumes wiping.

'How do you do.' Sadie's desperate to escape. They're so happy and relaxed together. 'Sorry, I've got to find someone. Have a good evening.'

She flees.

She can't seem to avoid them. She's shed her coat and is leaning on a poser table later, chowing down some excellent beef ragù with Valerie and an American influencer called Arianna Rodriguez. Arianna is in ecstasy over the ivy-print Astrid Carmichael table cloths they've had made to cover the tables.

'I'm sure we can nick you one,' Sadie tells her. 'I'll steal one for you later and you can sneak it back to your cottage. It won't be a problem.'

As she takes a swig of her drink—she's switched to vodka tonics in an effort to stay awake—she sees Ned and Caroline standing at a table just in front, with two people from the finance team. They're still laughing. Caroline says something and Ned tips back his head and belly-laughs. She's so entranced by this novel sight that she can't tear her eyes away from them. Caroline's ditched her coat too. Her dress is backless and over one glossy shoulder Sadie sees a huge tattoo that reminds her of a William Morris design. She wouldn't have expected Ned to have a tattooed girlfriend. Sign number two hundred and sixty-three that she's pigeon-holed him.

~

As the evening wears on, the ambiance shifts from what

Ned would have described as an elegant, stylish soiree to more of a traditional Christmas party. The poser tables are moved towards the edges of the room as people finish grazing, and the majority of the Oast House becomes a huge dance floor.

He's having a far better time than he would have imagined. The red wine has been going down well, and Caroline's on brilliant form. She's so blown away by the place that it's infectious, and he starts to see it through her eyes. Evelyn and her team have done a brilliant job with the decor, and Zoe's food is extraordinary as always. The mood is ebullient, and despite his endless moping after Sadie, he finds he's enjoying himself more than he has in a long time.

Unfortunately, Sadie's never far from his consciousness. She's wearing a dress so dazzling that she looks like an Oscar statuette. She's more golden than ever this evening: gold—tiny—dress, gold skin, her gorgeous blonde hair loose for one glorious night. The dress clings to her as if it was made for her and leaves little to the imagination. He knows he's biased, but she's a goddess. He can't take his eyes off her. She's turned the charm on full-blast tonight; he watches as she sparkles and laughs and converses. At least most of the attendees she's hosting seem to be female. Caroline begrudgingly confirms his opinion of Sadie's looks.

'I hate to say it, but she's absolutely bloody stunning. Ugh. Look at her boobs in that dress!'

'I really can't.' Ned averts his eyes. The last thing he needs for his sanity is to check out Sadie's incredible breasts any more than he has already.

'Beauty is only skin-deep, Ned. Is she still being a total bitch to you?'

He thinks back to her unprovoked rudeness in the

kitchen, and her sweetness the day his column was published.

'I don't like that word. But for the most part, yeah, she's pretty curt with me.'

'In that case, you're well rid of her. We'll have to get you on Tinder in the new year, but meanwhile, let's dance.'

The dance floor starts to fill up over the next hour, probably despite, rather than because of, their moves. The DJ is excellent and Ned feels himself breaking into a sweat. He's still in his work clothes; he wore a blazer and tie today for the occasion. He takes off his tie and unbuttons the top two buttons of his shirt. He needs to get rid of this blazer.

'I'll be right back,' he tells Caroline, and slips off the dance floor.

As he goes to find a chair to put his blazer and tie on, he spots Sadie coming towards the dance floor. She's on her own, and she's so luminous, it makes his heart hurt. He raises his hand in greeting. She sees him, and her eyes widen, and as if in slow motion he watches her take an almighty tumble.

She lands on her hands and knees; he's at her side in an instant.

'Shit.' He puts his hands on the soft skin of her upper arms. 'Are you ok?'

'*Fuck*', she says. Her head is bowed; she's crouched over. 'That fucking stings. *Ow*.'

'You poor thing,' he says. 'That looked nasty. Can you get up?'

He helps her to her feet.

She avoids eye-contact with him as she brushes dust off her hands. 'How mortifying. Jesus. I'm not even that drunk.'

'Don't worry about it.' He looks down at the floor. There's a mucky, wet slick where she landed. 'Looks like you slipped on some spilt booze. Could have happened to anyone. Have you cut yourself?'

He squats down. One of her knees is dirty and bleeding, thanks to the grit people have trampled in from outside. A trail of blood is already making its way down her shin. It needs a clean-up job and a plaster.

'There should be a first-aid kit in the front office.' He points towards the lobby. 'Think you can make it over there if I help you? I'll get you patched up.'

Her face twists. She looks as if she might cry. That bruised dignity over taking a fall never leaves you. He glances around and sees an unused napkin on a nearby table.

'Here.' He offers it to her, and she takes it and puts it to her knee. Then he offers her his hand, and she takes that too. He grips it.

'Come on,' he says. 'Let's get you sorted out and back on the dance floor.'

24

Sadie hobbles across the room, one hand holding the napkin to her knee, the other in Ned's resolute grip. The cut stings, and her dignity is bruised, but the high of being closer to him than she's ever managed before far outweighs both those issues. His shirt sleeve brushes the hair on her bare arm like caress after caress as he navigates them through the throng, and she's aware of his constant glances at her to ensure she's keeping up. He opens the door to the little office and storeroom by the loos and lets her pass through, closing it behind them.

'In here.' He pats the desk. 'Can you get up on this?'

She sits up on it and gingerly shimmies backwards to get more of her thighs on the surface without taking the pressure off her cut or letting her dress ride up too much. The din outside is muffled, and his massive physicality dominates the tiny space. She focuses on trying to quiet her breathing, which sounds as deafening to her as it did when she was a child, plastered behind some curtains, playing hide-and-seek.

'Ok,' he says. 'Hmm.' He strums his fingertips on the desk and looks around. 'If I were a first aid box, where would I be hiding?'

She watches as he opened a couple of cupboard doors.

'Bingo.' He really is such a dork. He has the dad-speak down pat. He'll make a great dad one day. *Don't think that. Don't think that.* He puts the first aid box on the desk and kneels down in the cramped space in front of her. 'Can I...?' he asks and goes to take the napkin. Now they're alone, she can smell the faint scent of chlorine, as well as the heavenly, herbal shower gel they use in the spa, and some other scent that's all his own, rising from him. She inhales as deeply and subtly as possible, before nodding and wincing as he carefully lifts the napkin off the cut. He grimaces and then looks up at her. His expression is one of gentle concern.

'I think it's best if I clean it first.' His gaze drops back to the cut. 'Are you happy to rest your foot on my leg, if I take your shoe off?'

He pats his thigh, and she swallows. *Am I happy? Fuck, yes.* It seems more appropriate to utter a polite *yes, thanks,* and she watches intently as he unfastens the delicate buckle of her sandal with meticulous care and slides it off. He's barely brushed her skin, but this tiny act feels thrillingly intimate. She puts her bare foot onto his thigh and encounters hard muscle beneath it. She squeezes her hands into fists to stop herself from wiggling her toes or, worse, running her foot up and down the impressive bulk of his quad.

He rummages in the first aid box and tears open a sachet containing an antiseptic wipe. He smiles at her as he unfolds it.

'I'll try to make this bit quick. Tell me if it hurts too much.'

As he bends his head and bites his lip in concentration, she watches in fascination, as absorbed in him as he is on the task at hand. This is the closest she's ever been to him; his face is six inches or fewer from her knee, and she has the strongest urge to ask him to just kiss it better. He puts his other hand tentatively around her calf and tightens his grip as he progresses with his cleaning task.

She couldn't have conceived of a scenario where he'd be bent over her, holding her leg. She soaks up the steady warmth of his exhales on her thigh and the pressure of his fingertips on her calf. His dark eyelashes fan onto his cheekbones as he cleans her up. It stings, but that's the least of her worries. This is agony. Karma is what it is. Payback for sleeping with a pregnant woman's boyfriend. Now she's found the man she actually wants to be with, and he belongs to someone else. Caroline is the one who gets to enjoy these hands on her at night and the pleasure of his shy smile.

As if he's read her mind, he looks up and rewards her with that same smile.

'You ok?' he asks. 'Not too painful?'

'It's fine,' she says, and then, because she's a masochist, she adds, 'Caroline seems nice.'

She can't help it; the word *nice* sounds strangled. He seems to catch the edge in her voice, and his smile increases as he wipes away the tiny river of blood that's trickled down her leg.

'She's very nice,' he says cheerfully. 'She's wonderful.'

She grits her teeth. 'How long have you guys been together?'

He looks up at her. 'Oh, God, no. We're not together.'

For once, she is genuinely dumbfounded. 'What do you

mean? I saw you at the Cenotaph together on Remembrance Sunday…'

'Did you? She's my brother's girlfriend. Jimmy—he's serving in Afghanistan. They've been together since they were kids; she's like a sister to me. He hasn't been granted leave for Christmas and she hasn't seen him for months; it's been really tough on her. So I brought her along tonight to give her a treat. She loves this place.'

Pressure leaves her body, whistling out of her ears and causing her shoulders to drop like a deflated balloon. Her jaw, which has been clenched, now aches to smile.

'So…' she presses on. 'You don't have a girlfriend?'

'Nope. Afraid not.' He busies himself with rummaging in the first aid box.

'But you told Nithya—the FT journalist—you did.'

'It seemed kinder than saying I wasn't interested.' He pulls out a plaster. 'I didn't want to hurt her feelings.'

'But she's beautiful.'

'I'm sure she is.' He flashes her a brief look and strips the backing off the plaster.

Everything is shifting, and a new potential reality is unfurling. Her vodka-relaxed brain scrambles to catch up. He is single. He is available. She knows he was interested at one point, but she's been so cold and hideous to him. Now the tables are turned, and she's desperate to know how he feels, but the ball is in her court. After the way she's acted, the first move has to come from her, and he'd be totally justified in humiliating her and telling her where to go.

A muscle in his jaw works as he hovers the plaster over her now-clean knee and slowly lowers it onto the cut. Their precious little window is sliding shut. His skin is creamy, and the perfectly kissable freckle on his cheek glints at her. His hair flops into his eyes and he brushes it away as he smooths the plaster down. It flops straight back down again.

She holds her breath, and puts out her hand, and gently combs the dark, silky strands of hair back off his forehead with her fingers, as her thumb brushes the soft skin at his temple.

She whispers one word. 'Ned.'

He looks up sharply, and she sees the dawn of realisation as he clocks the sincerity on her face.

'Are you serious?' he asks, but his tone is one of wonder rather than accusation.

She swallows and nods, her hand moving down his cheek of its own accord. It's far braver than the rest of her. Lustrous skin. The faintest beginnings of stubble under her fingertips. The sculpted infrastructure of his cheekbone and jaw draped in velvet.

'Now I know you don't have a girlfriend, I'm deadly serious. I really thought you were taken. But I've been a complete bitch to you, so I don't know if I've missed my chance.'

He shakes his head as if he can't believe what she's saying and lowers it, dropping a featherlight kiss onto her sore knee. His head hangs there for a moment, as if in prayer. Then he runs his hand reverently down her calf, fingers skimming her anklebones and, cupping her instep, gently removes it from his thigh. She shivers. He meets her eyes and smiles a beautiful, generous smile into them. It's a smile that speaks of bridges being built and doors being opened. He gets to his feet, standing in front of her.

'I can't believe it.' He's still smiling, but there's bafflement on his face, too. 'You avoid me like the plague. You could not be more dismissive or hostile if you tried.' As he speaks, he lifts a hand and slides it tentatively around her neck and she curls her head into it like a cat. He's watching her face as if he's expecting her to hiss and spit at him. She can't blame him, after the way she's acted.

'I had to be.' She hooks her fingers around his forearm. 'You were too much temptation. I promised myself after… that last fiasco that I wouldn't go near any guy who was in a relationship. No matter how much I wanted to.'

'You're kidding me. I just assumed you'd stepped your Princess Charmless behaviour up a notch. You bit my head off a few weeks ago, when I suggested drinks.'

She squirms. 'Sorry about that. I thought you had a girlfriend, and I didn't want a pity drink. I was terrified of what I'd do if I let myself have any contact with you, so I've been trying to stay the hell away.'

'Five minutes of conversation outside of work and you would have known I was single. Two minutes, even. But I get how it looked. I had no idea Nithya had fed back what I said, or that you'd seen me with Caroline. What a mess. I just thought you were a scary, hostile—'

'Bitch?'

He smiles. 'No. I was going to say motherfucker. If I'd known I had any chance at all, I would have persevered a lot harder, believe me.'

He moves the hand on her neck so that his thumb levers her jaw upwards. His other hand comes up to match it and his thumbs massage the underside of her jaw while his fingers acquaint themselves with her neck. She twists her head from side to side at the decadence of this warmth that infuses her skin and spreads downwards. Her eyes are fixed on his, and she watches as his face comes closer to her. His eyes are dark. The insanity of ever having felt indifferent to him hits her again.

He puts his mouth on hers: a light pressure; sublime softness; finally, the scent of his skin close enough for her to inhale him like a truffle hound. She parts her lips to let him in and runs her hands up over his arms and across his shoulders before hooking them around his neck. She encounters just what she imagined she would since that day at the pool: luxurious muscle. His delts make perfect domes, and the fabric of his shirt strains across his back as he bends down to her level. He makes a strangled, sighing noise low in his throat, and every muscle inside her clenches.

The kiss is all-consuming—tongues sliding and twisting and porcelain dings of teeth hitting teeth. She's becoming vaguely aware of getting a sore neck from leaning up to him when he runs his hands down the sides of her body and under her bum, pulling her up off the table. She wraps her legs around his waist and her arms tighten their grip on his waist. She's plastered to his front like a koala bear and she holds on for dear life.

He shifts his grasp of her so one of his arms is holding her up and the other is free to grab a handful of her hair. He pulls away just enough to say into her mouth, 'Relax. I've got you,' before sinking back into the kiss.

She's in a kind of stupor, kissing Ned Fitzsimmons. She wants lips on lips, tongues around tongues, skin on skin, forever. She wants to inhale the same air as him. She wants fistfuls of his glorious musculature. This mild-mannered man, who's been labelled *nice* by everyone in the office since she's met him, is currently behaving exactly as she's hoped he'd be capable of. He has his hands full of her too. His free hand roams up and down the length of her hair and her back. Her dress has ridden right up, and the fingernails of the hand supporting her weight dig into the flesh at the top of her thigh. She presses herself further into him and he groans.

He shifts his head. 'Can you stand up?' he whispers into her ear.

'I've only got one shoe on,' she says.

He snorts. 'Ok, Cinders. Give me a sec.'

He lowers her bum back onto the desk and kisses her on the mouth before kneeling once more.

'Still terrified?' he asks her, smirking. If he wasn't so *nice*, she'd think he was enjoying undoing her.

'Only of getting fired if anyone walks in on us.' Her eyes slide to the door.

'Angus and Evelyn don't have a leg to stand on in that department. Nor do Jess and Zoe.'

He picks up her sandal and slides it onto her foot, fiddling with the tiny buckle. When he's fastened it he looks up at her, and the intensity in his eyes makes her exhale sharply.

'I like this vantage point,' he says, and runs a hand up each of her bare legs. He strokes her knees in a circle and moves back down again. 'Mmm. Beautiful legs. Your skin… This dress is… I'm not capable of full sentences right now.' As he slides his hands slowly up and down her calves, he bends his head and presses his nose into the space where her thighs hollow out above her knees. 'Fuck,' he says in a muffled voice.

At the sound of his words and the sight of his head bent over her and the heat of his breath on her thighs, her heart melts and oozes and drips, running down through her torso in molten rivulets and pooling in her groin. She bends over him and slides her arms down his back, rubbing her face into his hair and kissing it. She sighs noisily into his hair.

He shifts, and she pulls back to let him sit up. He smiles up lazily at her.

'You okay?' His hands stroke her thighs.

'I'm a puddle on the floor. I'm in heaven.'

'I know what you mean. I could spend my whole life between your thighs.'

She giggles.

'Not like that,' he says. 'Well, yes like that, but also like this.'

He lifts his palms and scratches her thighs gently with his fingernails. Up and down. Up and down. She squirms and opens her legs slightly as her breathing gets more laboured.

His large hands are spanning her thighs now, his thumbnails tracing a non-existent inseam.

'I'd ask you to come home with me,' he deadpans, 'but I'd hate to bore you. I know how dull you find me.'

'I'll give you the benefit of the doubt.' She's gabbling. 'I'm not planning on letting you do much talking.'

He laughs. 'Such a little charmer, aren't you? What a delight.'

Her eyes follow him greedily as he stands up. For someone so huge, he's remarkably graceful. She lifts her face up to him as if she's a sunflower soaking up the sun, and he bends and kisses her again. When he straightens up, his eyes are shining.

'I can't get used to the idea that I'm allowed to do that,' he says. 'I've wanted to do it for so long—ever since I first saw you.'

A pang of guilt hits her in the stomach. 'You'd better get used to it.'

'I keep expecting you to give me a death stare, like I'm something you want to crush under that sexy little sandal. I definitely can't get used to you looking at me like you might actually tolerate me.'

'I'm looking at you like you're the best sight I've ever seen.'

'Interesting,' he says mildly, and trails his fingers down her upper arms. They erupt in goosebumps.

'Listen,' he says, and she tenses. 'We can't go home together tonight. I mean, you've got clients here, and it would be very poor form for me to ditch Caroline and run off with you. Besides.' He pauses and averts his eyes.

Panic seizes her. 'Besides what?'

'I don't want to just jump into bed with you without talking it through first. We have to work together, and if you were to revert to being Princess Charmless tomorrow morning, I don't think I could handle it.'

'I won't.' She's begging now; it's a low point, but she doesn't care. 'I'll be so nice, you won't even recognise me. Let me show you. I *need* to be with you.' She leans her head against his chest in despair and slides her hands around to his bum. It's rock hard under those awful diaper-butt chinos he's wearing.

'You're very dramatic.' There's amusement in his voice. 'Believe me, I'd love you to show me. But we've both had a few drinks, and I want us to think this through. Why don't you come over for supper after work tomorrow? Then we can have a chat.'

She lifts her head and gazes at him through her eyelashes. 'If I come over, can I stay the night?'

'If you've convinced me of your intentions,' he says drily.

She pouts. 'How am I supposed to get through the day tomorrow? Can I sit next to you at work?'

'That's a question I never expected to hear come out of that beautiful mouth. Of course you can. We can flirt.' He bends down and whispers in her ear; his fingers fiddle with her dress' tiny shoulder strap. 'It'll be *hot*. Any chance you can wear this dress to work?'

She presses her nose into his chest and sniffs. Shower gel. Chlorine. Him. The idea of spending the day beside him tomorrow is growing on her. She'll think of it as extended foreplay.

'No chance on the dress. And okay about tonight. I can't believe you're making me wait, but okay.'

'Poor impatient little chicken. I have no sympathy—I've had to wait a hell of a lot longer than you. You can handle another twenty-four hours.'

I've been waiting longer than you know, she thinks.

He holds her to him and rubs her back as she shamelessly gropes his bum. He's so delicious that her mouth is watering.

When he releases her, he looks down at her cleavage and sighs. 'I can't believe I'm saying no to a night with these. I must be crazy.'

She laughs delightedly. This dress of dreams has served its purpose and then some. 'You can have a feel. Something to keep you going.'

'That's not very gentlemanly,' he says, but he's looking at her as if he daren't hope she's serious.

'Ned. I have zero interest in you being a gentleman. Get that into your head. Now, do you want to grope me, or don't you?'

He puts out a hand and cups the underside of her breast, weighing it in his hand. Then the other hand; the other breast. The dress has a built-in balconette bra so she can't feel much, and she doubts he can either, but the look of tortured awe on his face is priceless.

'One more reason to let me stay tomorrow night, eh?'

She raises her eyebrows at him, and he shakes his head. 'I don't stand a chance against you.' He kisses her and trails his hands down to her waist to help her off the desk.

'One more thing,' he murmurs. 'I go for a swim on Friday lunchtimes. If you want to join me, bring your swimming costume in tomorrow. Thrashing it out in the pool helps with sexual frustration; take it from me.'

25

Sadie was convinced she'd be far too frustrated to sleep, but by the time she dragged herself away from Ned and showed the journalists some attention (in between desperate, longing glances at him), she was exhausted. She fell into bed after a quick cab ride home and gave begrudging thanks that she didn't have to perform. Ned does seem, irritatingly, to be the font of all wisdom.

Her excitement at seeing him this morning is working wonders on her hangover and tiredness. She showers and shaves her legs and blow-dries her hair with deadly focus. Into her tote bag she stuffs her swimming costume and make-up bag as well as her toothbrush and some clean underwear. She's determined to score an invitation to spend the night at Ned's. She'll be nice as pie and hot as hell, and she'll show him, with every glance and touch and word, how serious she is about him.

Last night started out as an utter bloody nightmare and escalated into something so wonderful that she can barely keep the wheel straight as she drives to the farm. Laser-sharp memories of his hands on her thighs and his tongue in her mouth flash up in her mind's eye. It seems he is hers. All her fuckwittery over the last few months hasn't been enough to make him run for the hills. Thank God he's more patient and loyal and forgiving than her.

When she walks into the office, her eyes go straight to him. It seems he's been keeping an equally sharp eye out for her, for he bobs his head above his screen and waves her over. As she walks around to his chair, he watches her as if she's descending from heaven. He's slicked his hair away from his face, and his smile is shy. She wishes with all her heart she could lean over and kiss him, and show him how ecstatic she is with the latest developments in their relationship. She compensates by giving him the most radiant smile in her arsenal.

'Good morning, Miss Thomas.' His smile grows in confidence in response to hers.

'Good morning.' She claps her hand on the coat and scarf thrown over the back of the seat next to him. 'Is this seat taken?' she asks flirtatiously.

'It is if anyone but you asks,' he says, standing up and grabbing his things. 'Let me take your coat for you. Revoltingly strong tea?'

'Please.' She cocks her head and slides out of her coat. He flashes his eyes down her body and back up before heading off with the coats.

As he sits back down and places her mug of perfectly made tea next to her, he whispers, 'Nice dress. Is that what they call a day-to-night number?'

She's worn a short black velvet shift with a white Peter Pan collar, and sheer black hold-ups. She's going for a sexy but virginal look on the outside, not in an attempt to mislead him on her sexual history (that ship has sailed) but to turn him on.

'You're such a dork.' She swivels in her chair to face him and leans forward. 'It's what they call an easy access number.' She gestures behind her. 'It has a zip down the back, or you can also get in this way.' She slides the hem up a fraction to reveal a hint of the lace top of her hold-up. 'I've tried to make things as easy as possible for you tonight. I'm *nice* like that.'

He puts his head in his hands and groans. When he looks up at her, his eyes are on fire. 'You don't have a nice bone in your body. It's going to be a long fucking day. I think I'm going to need a swim very soon.'

~

NED IS disinterested in every part of his job today. It's most out of character for him, but the beautiful blonde next to him sucks the air out of his lungs and has every one of his senses standing to attention. *Everything* has changed overnight—he sees the whole world with new eyes. On his dawn drive to work this morning, the bare trees looked majestic rather than stark, and he marvelled at the bleak beauty of the cold blue morning light. They are only two people among billions, but last night was his own personal miracle: the happiest few minutes of his life.

He can't quite believe he had the strength to send her home alone last night. To think he could have woken up entangled with her this morning! The idea of her warm, naked body curled into his, of flesh on flesh, makes him swallow and scoot his chair forward so his crotch disappears further under the table.

He stares at their year-end accounts with unseeing eyes

and instead replays that moment when he felt her fingers in his hair and looked up to see an expression on her beautiful face he'd never seen before, except for that brief moment by the pool: desire and intention. Up until that moment, the exquisite torture of having her satiny leg in his hands was almost too much to bear. He was right to send her home, though. He has to know; he has to see how she acts with him today, sober and at work, before he'll let them create memories that he'll never be able to get out his head.

He can't stop looking over at her and drinking in the pink, plump lips that were on his last night. He's immensely gratified that she seemed to feel the same way. She makes and receives a few calls, mainly with journalists who attended last night, but she is far twitchier than usual. Her gaze keeps sneaking to him and when it does, the look in her eyes makes him breathe harder and faster. Her pupils seem to dilate more every time he looks at her. He's looked at those eyes so many times over the past few months and now they're focused only on him. At eleven, she points upwards at the clock on the wall and mouths *only eleven o'clock!* She lets her head fall dramatically onto her keyboard and he laughs.

'Need to go thrash it out in the pool soon?' he asks her, his voice low and his expression neutral.

'I'd rather go and thrash it out in one of the cottages,' she groans. 'What are you cooking me tonight, anyway?

He ignores the innuendo and the unhelpful visual it conjures up. 'I have a secret weapon. She's called Zoe. She said I can pick up some Chicken Provençal from the kitchen later, if that works for you? I'd rather spend time entertaining my beautiful guest than slaving over the stove, to be honest.'

That seems to perk her up. She sits up and swivels

towards him. Her dress is puritanical from the waist up, but her face is pure renaissance: pale golden hair and those incredible navy-rimmed aqua eyes. Botticelli would burn to paint her. Her freckles have gone into hibernation for the winter, leaving golden uniformity.

'I would *far* rather you entertained me, too,' she says. 'I can't wait to see you in your natural habitat. Have you papered the walls with spreadsheets?'

'Ha ha. I'm just sorry I'm not taking you to a romantic restaurant. Next time.' He glances around the room and puts his hand on top of hers.

'Are you kidding me?' She drops her voice to a whisper. 'I don't want some random restaurant. You have no idea how much I want to be at home, at *your* home, with you. I want to see your little Ned-cave and sniff your bedsheets and poke around in your bathroom cabinet. I want the full Ned Fitzsimmons experience.' She drops her eyes to his waistband. 'The *full* experience.'

She's a piece of work. The concept of her standing in his home tonight—and possibly even lying in his bed—is so monumental it makes him break out in a sweat. It's all he's ever wanted, to take her home with him. He'll need to go and find respite in the pool soon.

~

THEY LAST another hour and then Ned suggests they slope off to the spa. Thankfully, no one else seems to be in a productive mood today—Lauren told Sadie earlier by the kettle that she'd vomited before she'd left the house. Most people are taking the whole of next week off for Christmas and have no intention of getting stuck into work today.

By the time Sadie has changed and wandered out of the

changing rooms into the indoor pool area, Ned is in mid-flow. She's in the black swimming costume that's slashed halfway down her torso, and her spray tan is holding up nicely. The memory of the heat in his eyes when he clocked her by the pool that day still makes her stomach flip. They have the place to themselves; she mentally punches the air, then watches him. He's doing front crawl this time, but once again he makes the pool look like a paddling pool as his body slices cleanly through the water.

She begins a leisurely breast stroke, keeping her hair dry. These blonde highlights are way too expensive to sabotage with chlorine. Ned seems to be doing three lengths for every one she manages. After a few lengths, she makes her way across the shallow end to lie in wait for him. He surfaces in front of her and stands up, grinning and pulling off his goggles. Good lord. He is *magnificent*. She looks on greedily as water runs over his pecs and down the line of hair that intersects his perfect comic-book-hero abs.

He squats and dunks himself and then runs his hands through his soaking hair, slicking it back off his face and giving her the full benefit of his V-shaped torso as the water pours off him in sparkling rivulets. It's an unconscious ritual he's probably performed a million times before at the end of a swim, and, because this is *Ned,* it's obvious he's not doing it for effect, but it's an utterly, perfectly wonderful sight—a spectacle for one. It deserves to be recorded, and replayed in slo-mo with some *Baywatch*-esque background music. It should be a gif. She wants to give him a standing ovation.

As he wades towards her, he throws his goggles onto the side of the pool and she licks her lips. She's actually salivating. *Get a grip, Sadie.* It's bizarre to think that the first time she feels his bare skin will be in a pool, and not in a bed. He squats in front of her. Before the poor guy has a chance to even think about escaping, she slithers into him like a malevolent sea creature and wraps her legs loosely around his waist, her hands going straight to the hallowed domes of his wet shoulders just above the surface of the water. His eyelashes are stuck together, and he blinks at her in lazy, starry-eyed wonder as water drips off the tip of his nose. He doesn't look too devastated to be entangled in her evil tentacles.

'Aren't you a sight for sore, hungover eyes.' His eyes dip to the deep slit at the front of her swimming costume, and his fingers trace a meandering line up the discs of her spine. 'And you're wearing my favourite swimming costume.'

She feels the vibration of a contented hum in her throat.

'Oh no,' she says. '*You're* the main attraction here. You're perfection.' She rubs her nose and lips along his cheekbone to his mouth. His skin is cool and damp, but the inside of his mouth is warm, and he draws her into a voluptuous, slow-moving kiss. She can't get close enough. She opens her mouth further and winds her evil tentacles more tightly around him. They are weightless and slippery and suspended, the silken water lapping around them. She wriggles into him and feels him harden against the gusset of her swimming costume, like a glorious taster of what's coming this evening. He made his exertions in the pool look effortless, but now his breath comes in sharp huffs.

'I like being practically naked with you,' she murmurs into his mouth. 'It's like I'm getting a sneak preview of tonight. I'm taking you for a test drive.' She punctuates her observation with a little tug of her teeth on his bottom lip.

'Mmm,' he manages. His hand massages her bum. 'Very presumptuous about tonight. What does madam think of this particular model, anyway?'

'At first glance, it looks very... top of the range. Very

robust. Nice, strong… gearstick.' She pushes down onto him and his laugh comes out more like a groan.

'Such objectification,' he tells her. No man has ever looked more thrilled at being objectified. His hand is taking its job of supporting her bum very seriously, and his fingers test the elastic of her swimming costume.

'Is this machine high performance?' Her hands acquaint themselves with muscle groups that seem as beautifully constructed and skilfully tuned as a Steinway.

'It's very powerful, madam. You wait and see.'

'That's encouraging.' She bends her head and intends to kiss the area between his neck and shoulder, but she finds herself slurping at his wet skin instead, as if he were a delicious, melting ice lolly. It would presumably be bad form to give her colleague a love bite, at least during the working day. Shame.

'The upholstery feels *amazing* against my skin,' she continues, her palms doing decadent laps of the sinewy path from his shoulders down to his wrists and back again. 'It even tastes delicious.'

'Glad to hear it, madam,' he says. 'You're the most delicious thing I've ever tasted.' And he silences her with his mouth for a few minutes until she finds the strength to pull away.

'My main concern is whether it's a smooth ride. I'll need to take it for a couple of spins to see if the experience is up to scratch. But I suspect it'll be a perfect fit for me.'

'You won't be disappointed, madam,' he whispers. 'You have my personal assurance.'

He gives her a smile so sweet and guileless that her heart begins to dribble through her insides again.

'I love your smile.' She cups his jaw in her hands. 'You're normally so serious at work.'

'That's because I'm very important.' He's still smiling at her.

'Dick.' She kisses her favourite freckle. It's too cute. She kisses it again.

'To be honest, I'm serious because I allowed my heart to be captured by a cold and charmless princess who couldn't have been less interested in me, so I haven't had much to smile about recently—until now.'

Her heart is properly unravelling now, spooling molten liquid down through her organs. She leans her forehead against his and presses the pads of her fingertips into his temples, as if she can make the pain she's caused him disappear. 'She sounds like a total bitch,' she says. 'You're too good for her.'

'No, I'm not.' His hand is on her jaw, holding her face up to his so she can see what his words and eyes are telling her. 'And I won't let anyone call her a bitch. She's incredible. And, I have reason to suspect she's actually quite charming, when she lets her guard down.'

'I think she owes you big-time. I hope you'll let her make up for being so shitty to you. You should let her quite literally charm the pants off you.'

'There's nothing to make up for. I just want to be with her. As I said, she's captured my heart. But if she wants to charm my pants off, I'll be delighted.'

'I promise you,' she says, 'your heart is in good hands. Any other organs she's captured, out of interest?' She rolls her hips lightly on him.

He groans. 'Oh yeah. My kidneys *adore* her.'

She giggles, and he gently brushes some stray hairs off her face.

'Now, as you can feel, I have a bit of a problem. I can't get out of this pool anytime soon.'

'Or do backstroke. You'd look like you had a periscope in those budgie-smugglers.'

'No, that would be a sackable offence, I'm pretty sure. Why don't you leave me to it, Princess Charming, and I'll swim off my frustration? On my front.'

26

Ned lives on a broad, tree-lined street in Sevenoaks that must be beautiful in summer. As Sadie rings his doorbell, she marvels at how grown-up his townhouse is, with its bay window, glossy black front door and plump wreath. Her stomach is flip-flopping like mad. It's ridiculous, given she's already kissed him twice and dry-humped him in the pool, but the stakes are high. She has to convince him that her interest in him goes far beyond one night together.

A shadow looms behind the frosted glass panes in the door, and he appears. He asked her to give him half an hour's lead time before following him home this evening and she was glad to. It gave her a chance to have a slightly hysterical giggle and gossip with Lauren, who was desperate to be distracted from her hangover with the details of their kiss, and to redo her face. She didn't have much makeup left on after her pool kissing session. The swim didn't dampen her ardour in the least; on the contrary, she spent the afternoon replaying how it felt to be coiled around Ned's body.

From the expression in his eyes whenever he looked at her, he was having the same problem.

He's changed. Gone are the boxy shirt and diaper-butt chinos, and in their place are a soft grey sweater and what look, at first glance, like socially acceptable jeans. Exciting. He holds out one hand and pulls her over the threshold, wrapping the other around the nape of her neck. As soon as his mouth is on hers, her apprehension dissipates a little. The pool session has emboldened him; there's no question embedded in this kiss. Instead, there is the certainty of ownership, and it's *hot*. Shy, uncertain Ned won her heart, but she's interested in seeing more of this new Ned, with a touch of the swagger he's long deserved. Presumably her shameless gyrating on him in the pool has given him reason to be confident in her feelings for him.

'You look beautiful,' he says.

'I look exactly the same as I've looked all day, with a bit more makeup.'

'Still beautiful. Come on in.'

He turns, and she checks out his arse. Yes. The jeans definitely showcase his assets far better than his unfortunate work attire, and the sweater skims his Batman shoulders. As her attention span widens beyond him, she sees that his hallway is painted a rich, womblike claret and smells gloriously of Zoe's cooking. She follows him through to a large, midnight blue kitchen that unfurls into a matching living room. Her first impression is of space and depth. The blue feels opulent but, at the same time, provides a neutral backdrop for Ned's treasures: at first glance, mainly books and art. A plump, fragrant Christmas tree stands in one corner, its lights twinkling softly.

'White ok to start?' he asks, offering her a wine glass and brandishing a bottle.

'Lovely, thanks,' she says, and, glass in hand, paces around the room, full journalistic mode engaged. This space tells her *so* much about this man.

'This is fascinating, seeing you in your natural habitat,' she tells him. 'I need to snoop; I'm about to go full David Attenborough on you.'

He shoots her an amused grin. 'Knock yourself out, Dave,' he says indulgently. 'What can you tell me about myself?'

She stops pacing and slowly turns full circle.

'You're full of surprises. One word. Roots.'

'Elaborate.'

'At work, you don't seem to care about *things* very much, except maybe gadgets. You wear the same uniform every day. I'd imagine your laptop is your most treasured possession. But somebody here has done some curating. This isn't the result of a quick trip to Ikea. It's beautiful. You've really made a sanctuary for yourself—you've invested; you've put down roots.'

The art on the wall is varied, from what she can see in the dim light. A huge blue and white abstract piece in the kitchen. More traditional oils in the living room, but still fresh: vibrant smears of colour laid unapologetically on with a knife, conjuring up British seascapes and landscapes. Wall-to-wall blue bookshelves stuffed with books. There is nothing sparse about the space, but every book and cushion look as though they've earned their place: every piece is intentional. Framed photos lean against book spines and stand on the mantlepiece. They all look like family photos; there are plenty of Ned with a guy who must be Jimmy, and Caroline features in several too.

She contrasts his home with the bland modernity of George and Lucy's flat, which is a step up from Ikea, but not much. She could pack up her room in ten minutes and be gone. No roots there. There weren't many roots at her flat share in Muswell Hill, either. She spent so much time at David's minimalist-flash apartment in the City that she didn't make an effort at her end.

Meanwhile, Ned has clearly spent a considerable amount of time creating a beautiful home and furnishing it with the things that feed his soul. She runs her fingers down the cracked spines on his bookshelves. He doesn't give much of himself away at work, and from that she inferred that there wasn't much to get to know. She took one look at him and wrote him off as a one-dimensional caricature, when the spines of these classics, and thrillers, and literary works of art tell her a different story. She is ashamed of herself. She's a journalist, and yet she took a subject at face value. But for a couple of lucky chances, she wouldn't have had an inkling of what lay beneath Ned's surface. Forget seeing him in the pool that time with Lauren; it was Nithya's decent journalism that opened her eyes to him.

She turns away from the bookshelf to face him. 'Your home is beautiful,' she tells him softly. 'It makes me realise what an enjoyable process it's going to be, getting to know you. I've just got to the tip of the iceberg.' The books are a reminder that it takes a lifetime to get to know someone else intimately. Each book stands for a single decision he's made to educate or entertain himself. Each book is a facet of Ned and his Ned-ness, and unwrapping the wonder of his Ned-ness, book by book, kiss by kiss, and conversation by conversation, will be her new passion. It may even be her life's work.

The look in his eyes is too much for her, like his emotions are splitting his chest open. He reaches her in a couple of steps and pulls her to him. She wraps her free arm around him and buries her face in his sweater, suctioning in its scent: chlorine again, *obviously*, and firewood, and body wash. If anyone had told her that the smell of swimming pools would one day cause her stomach to flutter, she'd have laughed. Her free hand spans a small fraction of the expanse of his ribcage, and it shudders under her palm as he breathes.

'Do you put down roots, beautiful Sadie?' he whispers into the top of her head. His voice is barely audible. Beautiful Sadie is far superior an endearment to Princess Charmless.

'I've managed to avoid it so far.' She attempts to laugh it off. 'I've even uprooted myself to come down here, for God's sake.'

'And do you still despise Sevenoaks?'

'Put it this way. I like it a lot more than I did yesterday,' she mumbles into his sweater, and his arms envelop her even more tightly.

'We'll find you some roots,' he says huskily.

~

EVERYTHING about her is softer than he expected. At work, she's clipped and disdainful. The armour she's built for herself is impenetrable. But here, in his home this evening, she's gentle and accessible. It seems she left her defences at the door of that tiny office last night, when, with one small movement of her hand in his hair, she built a bridge across a chasm he thought was uncrossable. There's banter tonight, but it's affectionate rather than competitive.

He has no words for how it feels to see her standing in his home. She'd be horrified if she knew how much time he's spent imagining her here. So many evenings, her ghost has stood next to him while he cooks, and has laid her head on his shoulder as he reads on the sofa, and has permitted him to curl himself around her in his bed. Now, in what feels like a miracle of quantum physics, she's materialised as a beautiful, flesh-and-blood goddess, in his kitchen. Not only that, but she's lit up. Her eyes glow an astonishing shade of pale blue, the pendant lights burnish her hair in a million shades of gold, and her dimpled smile captivates him. She's no ghost: his fantasies of her were so insubstantial compared to the impact of her physical presence.

He feeds her at the island: Zoe's chicken, and a tart green salad, and roasted sweet potatoes. A light, silky Burgundian pinot to wash it down. He watches as she swirls and sips; he soaks up the appreciation on her face when the wine hits the back of the throat. Every second he doesn't have his eyes fixed on her is a second wasted. Everything he does is to earn a smile and buy himself another glimpse of those dimples.

As they eat, the conversation flows easily. They talk about work, about how fortunate they both feel to have landed in the nest of somewhere as special as Sorrel Farm, and about what it is about Jess, Zoe, Evelyn and Angus that inspires such unwavering loyalty in their employees. They talk about homes, and he confesses that Caroline's mum, an interior designer, did a lot of the heavy lifting in pulling this place together. And then, over the rich chocolate *torte* Zoe pressed on him, they talk about relationships, or more precisely, they cover Natalie and Sadie's ex, David.

From what she says, it sounds as though there was very little intimacy in her relationship. He discerns that there was little keeping them together beyond the superficial glamour their careers afforded them. David sounds like a twat. That Sadie could be little more than a high-value trophy for some City boy to show off along with his Lotus makes his heart rate quicken.

Intimacy is everything for him. It was what made letting Natalie go so hard, even though he didn't love her enough to see a future with her. He's missed the intimacy far more than he's missed her specifically—he's missed washing another person's skin, wrapping himself around another body and picking another person's half-read book off the floor. But intimacy without love is a false comfort, and it leaves a bitter taste; it taunts you with its inadequacy.

He looks at the spellbinding woman sitting next to him, the woman whose slender limbs were wrapped around him in that blissful pool session today. This proximity with her is more than he could have dared to dream of twenty-four hours ago, but he wants more. He wants true intimacy with her: to know every move and sound and idiosyncrasy that makes her Sadie, instead of being familiar only with the tightly packaged persona she allows him to witness at work.

She looks up from her wineglass and catches the expression in his eyes. He probably looks psychotic as he plots how he can keep her here with him for as long as possible. Her face softens, and she reaches over with her free hand and strokes her thumb down his cheek.

'I'm so obsessed by this freckle,' she says.

He's taken aback. 'What freckle?'

'You have a little freckle right here.' She presses her thumb pad into the centre of his cheek. 'It's so delicious, it makes me drool. It's become, like, a beacon in my life. The past few weeks, I just kept thinking about how much I wanted to kiss that beautiful little freckle. Looking at it makes my heart break.'

He's touched beyond words that she's been feeling like this—especially about a freckle that he had no idea existed.

He clasps her hand and brings the palm to his mouth, pressing a soft kiss onto it before closing up her fingers and wrapping both his hands around it.

'I feel the same about your dimples. Every day, my aim is to get to see those dimples in action. Most days, I fail; all I get is death stares, but sometimes someone else makes you smile when I'm around and it makes my day. The first time I saw them was on your very first day, in the Oast House, when that dick, Danny, was chatting you up. Your face lit up in a smile and I just thought, *wow*. You're even more of a knockout when you smile.'

Her face crumples as if she's on the verge of tears.

'Hey.' He's still holding her fisted hand. 'I didn't mean to upset you; I'm so sorry.'

'It's not your fault. It's just—ugh—I still feel so awful about that whole episode. I wish it had never happened. His poor girlfriend.'

'I'm sorry if he hurt you,' he says carefully.

'He didn't hurt me—not really. I was more mortified than devastated; I was shocked that I'd been such a bad judge of character. And I was really fucking angry for his girlfriend. But more than anything, I just wish I'd come to my senses about *you* earlier.'

Her eyes are seriously intense, like she really wants to make him understand something. She pulls her hand out of his grasp and slides her palm around his neck. He's falling into her eyes, mesmerised. Once again, it hits him how surreal it is to finally have this magical creature here, in his home, gazing at him, her hands on him.

'I know you said last night you wanted to have a chat before we went any further.' Her soft, slim hand strokes his neck. She's not short, but her bone structure is very fine. Everything about her is refined and delicate—except for that death-stare of hers. Right now, the way she's looking at him is the precise opposite of her death-stare. She's staring at him as if she's committing every one of his features to memory.

He shifts on his stool. 'I didn't want to rush things. I've waited too long to be with you to risk misjudging what you want here. While I can't believe you're actually interested, on any level,'—he flashes her a grin, to communicate how ecstatic he is about this development—'I can't spend the night with you if this is just a onetime thing you need to get out of your system.'

She's still staring at him with those crazy eyes. She's shaking a little.

'Ned.' Her words tumble out. 'This is *not* a onetime thing. No fucking way. I want as much of you as you'll give me. I'm not about to mess you around. If anything, you've got the power here. You know I can be a nasty little pain in the arse, and you're such a good person—you're an amazing person. You work so hard and you're decent to everyone. I don't want to tarnish you with my... brattishness.'

He laughs at the last label, and the vague tension he's felt all night leaves his body as she articulates what he's dreamt of hearing. *I want as much of you as you'll give me.* Her pull is too strong. The perfume she wears is something he's snatched brief wafts of at work; last night he wallowed in it when he kissed her and it's drifting around him tonight too—she smells of jasmine. He leans into her and kisses her. It's awkward, kissing on the barstools, so he gets up and wraps his arms around her. He can show her more eloquently with his kiss than with words that she can have as much of him as she wants. She already has it. She's had it since she walked into the office for the first time.

It's not a polite kiss, not the kind of kiss he'd normally go for after dinner with a woman, but she's given him all the reassurance he needs and she's asked him for reassurance in return. This kiss is urgent: mouths wet, breath hot, lips sliding, tongues taut and twisting. His hands move across the fabric of her dress and down over her sheer stockings. He's memorising the way her body feels under him. She sighs into his mouth and it feels like relief.

'You're my absolute favourite brat,' he tells her, and he pulls back enough to see her dimples flash in response.

27

When she smiles at him, his eyes drop to her mouth and he glides his mouth across hers, from dimple to dimple, before he hones back in on her lips and begins to kiss her again with renewed purpose. Her points of focus narrow to the rhythmical slide of his tongue in and out of her mouth and the fierceness with which he's massaging the side of her thigh, just above her stocking top. Right now, nothing else exists apart from the smell and the taste and the feel of this man. She cocks her head and twists her tongue in his mouth, and he catches it lightly between his teeth. Her skin is prickling with sweat under her dress, and the ache inside her comes out as something between a whimper and a moan.

He seems to be struggling too. He pulls away enough to say shakily, 'I think I'm going to need to get you out of this outrageously sexy little dress soon.' He runs a finger under the stiff, high collar and shakes his head. 'Ridiculous,' he says to himself.

She arches her body towards him. 'Yes please,' she begs

him, and then remembers her manners. 'Shall we wash up first?'

He looks around as if he's forgotten about the inconveniently dirty plates, and gives her a grin that is most definitely not suggestive of washing up.

'No fucking way. I'll just soak them.'

He pulls away from her and plugs the sink, running the tap and chucking the casserole dish and plates in with what she suspects is a most un-Ned-like lack of precision.

He leads the way upstairs and makes his way through a darkened room to flick on a bedside lamp. As he heads around the bed to the second lamp, she takes an appreciative look around. It's a large room, painted a taupe worthy of a boutique hotel. Weirdly tidy. Huge bed. Zero clothes strewn on bed or floor. Crisp, white linen that's beautifully pressed. Thank God. He's a keeper. There's nothing worse than guys with grungy, coloured bed linen that turns out to have some synthetic content.

'Are you always this tidy?'

He smiles. 'Cleaners came today. You lucked out.' He strolls towards her in a manner that reminds her of a large desert cat approaching its prey: leisurely; purposeful. It's very, very sexy.

'I have *the* Sadie Thomas in my bedroom,' he says, arms sliding around her waist and down over her backside. His smile broadens until he's positively beaming, and her heart swells as if it's synchronised with his smile. This man is too much; he's the best of humanity in beautiful gift-wrap.

'I can't believe you're here.' He brushes his lips across her forehead and bunches up the back of her dress. The fabric slithers over the nerve-endings of her bum and she shivers.

'I hope you're not in a hurry,' he whispers, 'because I want to enjoy every moment of this. And, may I just say, you have the finest arse it's ever been my privilege to feel up.'

She doesn't have words for him right now. The intimacy of standing alone with him, in his heartbreakingly tidy bedroom, hearing nothing but their breathing and the friction of fabric on skin, is extraordinary. It's lighting her up from inside out. God knows what she'll be like when their clothes are shed and skin moves against skin. She lays her hands on his upper arms and rubs her nose into his neck, soaking up as much of his skin as she can. It's not enough. She gives his neck a little lick and he shudders.

As she pulls away, she looks up at him and her eyes tell him *come on*. He releases her bum and slides his hands up to her shoulders and turns her around. Her hair's tied back, as usual, and his breath hits the bare nape of her neck in warm puffs. She feels the tug of her zipper coming down, slowly, slowly, to just below her bra hooks, before he gently parts the open neck of her dress and cool air hits her skin. One hand slides around to her stomach and pulls her to him. She covers it with her hands. The warmth of his palm radiates through her dress, and the heat flows outwards over her abdomen. Then she inhales sharply through her teeth as he begins to kiss and lick her skin, moving lazily down from her neck and over the discs of her spine.

He sighs raggedly into her back. He pulls his hand away from her stomach, and her dress loosens around her as he unzips it as far as it'll go. She's expecting him to slide it off her shoulders, but he slips a hand inside the opening at the back and curls it around her waist until it's back on her stomach, rubbing her bare skin in circles as her muscles contract in need. She gasps, and he doesn't sound like he's doing too well behind her; he makes noises like he's in pain as his lips and other hand travel down her back towards the top of her thong.

She reaches behind her and attempts to squeeze his bicep. It doesn't yield. 'Don't pass out on me back there,' she says.

'You're killing me.' His voice is hoarse. 'Not sure I'll survive long enough to finish the job. I can't even handle your back.'

'Don't even think about it,' she warns, and her voice shakes as his hand dips down over her knickers at the front. 'Man up; come on, Ned.'

He laughs. 'You're a delight, as always. I'll be strong.'

His voice is behind her right ear now, and he nips it with his teeth as he finally slides off her dress. She tugs the sleeves down and it pools around her on the floor.

He lets out a strangled version of *God* as he checks out her body from behind before pulling her back against him, his hands spanning her hip bones. She instantly feels his hardness through his jeans and spins around. There are still far too many layers of clothing between them.

He looks at her as if he's shell-shocked, as if he can't trust the messages his eyes are sending to his brain. He glances down at her black bra and thong and then catches her eye again, allowing himself to break into a smile as he shakes his head at her.

'This is already the best night of my life,' he says. 'I can't even process how beautiful you are. In all my sad, lonely fantasies about doing this with you, I still didn't get it right; you're more extraordinary than I could have imagined. This skin…' He smoothes his hands over her shoulders and down her arms and his voice trails off.

So he had fantasies about her. She would have guessed he had, of course. After all, she's had plenty about him. But hearing him say it, right here in his bedroom, is exceptionally gratifying.

'I've had sad, lonely fantasies about you, too.' She won't admit to getting herself off after seeing him at the pool. Well, not yet, anyway. Maybe she'll tell him next time. He'll definitely enjoy that anecdote. 'Now, get this bloody sweater off. I want to see how accurate they were.'

He pulls it off over his head, and there he is. Skin. The relief of it is extraordinary. This isn't like being in the water, which smoothed and glossed over every touch and dialled down their sensations. Now his skin is warm, dry, scented, the smattering of hair across his chest and down over his stomach lighter than when it was wet. She fans out her fingers and moulds her palms to the curves of his pecs and presses her face into his breastbone, inhaling him properly now. This beats sniffing him through his clothes. Her hands slide down over his glorious torso and around to the satiny skin of his back, and she holds him to her as tightly as she possibly can, turning her face so her cheek is glued to his chest, but it's not enough.

He can see what she's trying to do, and he helps her, his arms tightly around her. He seems to be able to span most of her back with his palms. He's breathing hard and his fingers fidget with the clip of her bra. She pulls back and grins at him.

'Go for it. They're all yours.'

His smile is blinding. It's as if she's just told him to fill his boots in a sweet shop. He fumbles for a second before the back of her bra springs open and he edges it off her shoulders and down her arms. He devours her with his eyes for a moment and pulls her back in towards him, and nothing has ever felt more right than the way her bare breasts feel against his abdomen. She does a luxurious little shimmy in his arms, basking in the friction his skin offers her nipples. His belt buckle is prodding her in the stomach. It's not the only thing prodding her. She needs to get these jeans off. Right now, with his hair falling over his eyes and that glorious happy-trail of hair disappearing into the top of his very distorted jeans, he looks like an X-rated version of a nineties Calvin Klein ad.

Now it's her turn to feel like a kid in a sweet shop. She makes a little purr of delight as she unbuckles his belt and undoes his jeans, and he laughs and winces as she edges them over his erection.

'Be gentle with me, Princess,' he says. 'I'm already a broken man.' But his eyes are dancing and flicking over her body as she works.

He helps her get his jeans down and kicks them off. They're down to their pants and she presses into him. His skin and the stretchy cotton of his boxers are so soft, and underneath he's rock.

'Bed,' he whispers, and the sheer adoration in his eyes as he lays her down on the cover puts pressure on her throat. They both seem to have some stubborn notion that the other only wants them for their body, but this isn't merely physical. She wants to get so close to him that she can climb inside him.

He lies on his side next to her, propped up on an elbow. Her ponytail is digging into her; she pulls off the band and shakes out her hair.

'This hair...' he murmurs, putting his leg over so he's straddling her. He entwines his fingers with hers and pins her arms above her head and smiles down at her before spending a few moments rubbing his face in her hair. 'Golden. That's what I thought as soon as I saw you.' He kisses words across her jaw to her mouth. 'So. Fucking. Golden. So. Heavenly.'

She opens her mouth and all he allows her is the most fleeting touch of his tongue to hers before continuing his journey downwards. She's a dead weight and light as a feather all at once. The suspense of what he'll do is hotter than she could have imagined.

He lowers his mouth onto her right nipple and flicks it with his tongue. A flash of heat streaks straight to her groin; she jolts and gasps at the same time as he chokes *fuck*. He goes to work on her breast, teasing her with featherlight kisses between rolling her nipple around and sucking on it. He takes it between his teeth with the lightest possible touch and runs his tongue over it and she bucks violently and raises her hips to grind against him. This is glorious, unspeakable torture. They both still have their pants on, for Christ's sake. Ned's hips respond to hers and roll against her, but she can't get her legs apart to feel him where she needs him.

'Ned', she says, and pulls her hands out from under his. Her voice sounds unfamiliar and guttural in her ears. She scrabbles at the waistband of his boxers. 'I can't wait; I can't. I need you now.'

He surfaces and puts his nose to hers. 'I'm only just getting started,' he says, smiling at her. 'You are so, so beautiful. Your nipples are insane. I haven't even got to the other one yet. And I want to taste you. I can hold on, if you can.'

A most unwelcome memory of Danny flashes in her mind's eye. That was a quick fuck, even if she didn't want to admit it at the time. This is most definitely not. He wants her here with him for the whole night and beyond, she can tell. She needs him to know she could spend the rest of her life in this bed with him, that she's not trying to rush him.

'Sorry,' she says breathlessly. 'Keep going. Just take it as a compliment.'

'Don't ever be sorry.' He kisses her so lightly and tenderly on the lips that her eyes prick. 'I'll go slow.'

And he does. He lavishes her with attention as he takes a trip around her body. Never has there been a more reverent tourist. He kisses and licks and caresses and massages, whispering words of adoration as he goes. He returns to her nipples every couple of minutes and she trembles, but for the most part his efforts to relax her pay off and she begins to drift into an altered state of bliss.

At last, he slides her thong off, and the sensation of the last fabric barrier leaving her body feels sublime. His expression as he gazes down on her is priceless: disbelief dissolves into intent. As soon as he touches her, she's incapable of speech, though her eyes can't leave the view of this beautiful man, kneeling between her legs, doing exactly what she's dreamt of him doing since she came to her senses. It's wondrously hot to watch him put his fingers on and in her, and it's even hotter to see the arousal playing across his gorgeous features.

'You weren't lying,' he tells her. 'You're so ready, it makes my head explode.'

He crouches down. When his mouth moves on her, it feels as though any remaining blood drains away from her brain and pools at the point where his tongue is exploring her with licks and laps and whirls. He breaks off to tell her he could never have imagined how incredible she would taste and then gets back to the job. As in the office, he's conscientious and detail-oriented and purposeful, and this time she really has no ability to stall any further. She stretches and tightens and spins into the vortex, and she snaps, crying out into her exhales and grabbing at his shoulders, urging him to come up and join her as she drifts back down to earth.

He crawls up the bed and wraps himself around her as she shudders into him, her face in his chest.

'I can't believe you,' he says. 'I thought you were beautiful before, but seeing you like this…' He breaks off and drops kisses onto her hair.

'Now it's your turn,' she tells him shakily. 'I really, really can't wait any longer. I need you. Now.'

He laughs and jumps off the bed and tugs down his boxers. He's divine.

She writhes on the bed. 'Come the fuck *on*, for fuck's sake,' she tells him, and he explodes with laughter.

'Charming as ever. Ok, Princess. I'll put you out of your misery.'

He opens his bedside drawer and pulls out a condom wrapper, which he tears open and rolls on. She stares at him as if she's going to eat him.

'Wow,' he says. 'You look like a starving puppy.' He climbs onto the bed and she scrambles out of the way and puts her hands on his shoulders to push him onto his back.

'I'm a puppy who needs a nice juicy boner,' she replies as archly as she can while she swings a leg over to straddle him, and she's rewarded with a blinding smile.

'I'm pretty sure princesses aren't supposed to speak like that,' he whispers. He's staring, watching to see what she'll do. She wraps her fingers around him, getting her first glorious feel of him, even with the bloody condom on. She guides him inside her and eases herself down, and they both gasp at the fit: so snug that the intensity hits her smack in the chest and her skin flickers with a light sweat. She wants to learn him, research him, earn a doctorate in him. She rolls her hips lightly, and the increased sensation is mirrored on his face. His long eyelashes flicker and his gorgeous lips part.

He presses his hands over her hipbones. 'Best view I've ever, ever seen.'

'View's pretty special from up here, too,' she assures him. She bends, trailing her nipples over the soft, ticklish hair of his chest until her mouth hits his. He made her wait; it's payback time. She kisses him languorously, luxuriously, and he groans into her mouth as he reciprocates with admirable enthusiasm.

After a while, she takes pity on him and starts to move her hips oh-so-slowly up and down, as far as she can without pulling him out of her completely. The friction as she empties herself of him and then fills herself up again is so heavenly it's making it hard for her to formulate any thoughts, let alone sentences.

His eyes have a pleading, drowning look in them that only someone very cold-hearted could ignore. His hips start to move more, meeting hers whenever she lowers herself back down onto him. She picks up her pace and wiggles her hips to get him as deep as possible inside her. They're in the perfect dance now, flawlessly in sync. She bends forwards, and he pulls her in for a deep kiss with a hand around her neck. His breathing is ragged, and he's filling her even more, if that's possible.

She sits back. This is too good to miss. As they move together, he holds up his hands, and she puts them on her breasts and covers them with hers. He looks at her, beseeching, begging for mercy, and she grinds down, hard. He bucks and falls and his body twists, and when she's confident he's spent she collapses on him, quads burning and energy expended and every fibre of her being clamouring to be close to this man, in this refuge they've made with their bodies.

28

She surfaces from the abyss of sleep, cosseted by the immediate understanding that the world is a better place today. She's consummated her fledgling relationship with Ned, turned what they have from ephemeral potential to technicolour fact.

The edges of his curtains glow with a grey dawn, but the room is still dark. The bed is outrageously comfortable and cosy. Her body feels slack and her mind vacant in a way she hasn't enjoyed in months. An earth-shattering orgasm will do that for you. Maybe she should bottle him and make him available on prescription.

He's right behind her, curled up against her like the softest shadow. Perhaps it wasn't just the orgasm. Perhaps his body has been feeding her a steady dose of endorphins while they've been asleep, skin to skin, like a giant nicotine patch. As they fell asleep last night, he told her he couldn't wait to wake up and do it all again. She'll take him at his word: she runs her hand over the forearm laid across her waist and the sole of her foot up his hairy, muscular calf to rouse him. Sure enough, he shifts and his arm tightens around her. She nestles further into him, pressing her bum backwards into the curve of his body, and it takes a gratifying whack as his erection springs to life.

Yes. She's going to show him her favourite thing: leisurely, semi-comatose morning sex. She reaches behind her and lazily strokes the skin of his hip, his thigh, then back around to his bum, pulling him towards her. He understands perfectly and joins her effort to fuse themselves together, his arm moving higher, pressing into her collarbones before gliding down again to brush her nipples. She whimpers at the pleasure of it, but he continues his travels down to her stomach. There's something about his big, warm hand on her stomach, his fingers splayed out across her skin and the light pressure he exerts to hold her close to him, that moves her. It's as if his hand has healing powers, and it's sending messages of security and wellbeing that travel through her skin and via her veins to flood her entire nervous system. When she's here with him like this, she's safe. She's untouchable.

They stay like that, suspended for a moment. He sighs into the back of her neck and she suspects he feels it too. Then his hand resumes its travels and edges between her legs, and her biochemistry obligingly flips: security to adventure. Her breathing quickens. She opens herself up to him, raising her top leg and planting her foot behind the crook of his knees. By edging her hips forward an inch or two, she can fit her hand into the space between them. His whole body stiffens as she takes hold of him and squeezes. She runs her fingers up and down his length, brushing the moisture at his tip with her thumb and weighing his balls in her hand before resuming her firm grip on him. She can feel the effect she's having on him, but his fingers remain unfazed, tracing tiny circles on her that bring her higher and higher.

They're both breathing like they're in a low-budget dirty movie, and it's the only sound she can hear apart from the slide of skin on skin. She can't see him, and they haven't spoken. It's beyond erotic. Unfortunately, needs must. She breaks her silence.

'Condom,' she manages.

He plants an open-mouthed kiss on her shoulder and twists away from her, and a cold chasm opens up under the duvet that makes her yelp. But he's back in seconds, foil ripping, latex snapping and a cap popping open. He eases his arm around her again, and she scoots back into the protective shell his body makes around her. He's found some lube—the cold gel is a rude shock on a part of her body that's currently ablaze, but the slipperiness with which his fingers slide around her and inside her makes her gasp. She raises her leg again.

He nudges inside her, tentatively at first and then, as she yields easily, with more force. Oh, God. *This* is what was missing. She's perfectly happy now; he's curled around the outside of her body and he's filling her up from inside, too. She's full of him and he's full of her. He begins to move slowly, rhythmically. Despite her ineffectual thrusts, he has to do the vast majority of the work in this position and he's fulfilling his responsibility nobly. God knows what groups of muscles he has to use to keep up this momentum lying on his side, but his insane swimming habit is clearly paying dividends. He doesn't have much leverage, but the thrusts are full and even, and he's hitting that elusive point inside her. He holds her to him and presses down hard on her stomach with the flat of his hand, ramping up the intensity inside her.

The swelling, expansive feeling of pressure builds and builds and turns her inside out until she falls apart, gripping his forearm and pushing against him as hard as she can. She's just drooled on his high thread-count pillow. He's still moving inside her, but she suspects he's been holding out for her to come, because he emits a low roar as he goes rigid and shudders, his head in the crook of her neck, kissing her jaw and shoulder feverishly.

She hooks her arm back to cradle his head in her hand. She thought she was vacant and spent when she woke up: she's a rag doll now, good for nothing except showing this man what he means to her. She pulls up her pelvis, wincing as she eases him out so she can roll over in his arms. She throws a leg over his thigh and comes face to face with him. His face is creased and unguarded, and in his beautiful eyes shine affection and wonder. Her heart is dribbling down through her innards again. Her smile is slow, sated and awash with emotion.

'Hello, you,' she says.

'Hello, yourself.' He smoothes a finger along her eyebrow. His eyes roam over her face. 'You ok?'

'I'm wonderful, but you've ruined me. You've shagged me senseless.'

She leans forward and touches her nose to his, then kisses his mouth. Featherlight. His freckle. Mmm. His mouth again, this time with a hint of tongue. He moans sleepily, but his eyes are open, and they gaze at each other. He opens his mouth and his hand bunches in her hair. Just the two of them, under the covers. The infinite miracle of human skin on human skin. She closes her eyes.

Ned cranks the handle downwards, and the shower springs to life. While it's warming up, he grabs a second towel and his spare, clean bathrobe from the airing cupboard and puts them on the towel rail. He pops his head around the adjoining door to the bedroom.

'Shower's ready.'

She pushes back the bedclothes and swings her legs out of the bed. She walks towards him, naked. He tries not to look, but he does. He tries not to grin, but he does. She's so ridiculously beautiful—the woman of his dreams—and here she is, padding across his bedroom floor after the best morning sex he can remember. She swipes his arse as she saunters past him, her side-eye swivel accusing and amused.

'Stop perving.'

He holds his hands up. 'Impossible. Sorry.'

The shower is boiling, and steam rushes out when he opens the cubicle door and ushers her in. He pulls her to him and they duck under the torrent of water together. They simultaneously suck their breath in through their teeth as they adjust to the heat raining down over their skin.

Her face burrows into his chest to avoid the downpour. Her arms slip around his waist. He holds her tighter and breathes into the top of her head as the water cascades over both of them. Everything he does with her feels special, loaded. Swimming. Eating. Showering. He can't imagine a time where hanging out with her would feel pedestrian. And being inside her was so out-of-this-world amazing that he's addicted: nothing else is good enough for him now. He's no longer content to gaze at her or work on earning a smile; he wants all of her.

She looks up at him as best she can, given the water streaming over her face, and her eyes shine with something more than plain affection. She reminds him of a cat who was previously disdainful and hostile. Now she purrs and slinks and rubs herself up against him. Everything about her is softer: her gaze, her tone, her demeanour. That arch dismissiveness she does so well has been laid aside and she looks younger, more vulnerable, more—open. She's let him in, and it's his turn to feel like a cat as he basks in the warmth of her favour.

She opens her mouth to say something and then smiles and looks away.

He strokes her wet hair back from her face. 'What?'

'Last night was amazing. This morning was—amazing.'

'Agreed. You are the best Christmas present ever.' He reaches behind her for the shower gel and squirts some into his palm. He rubs his hands together and begins to smooth the lather over her shoulders and down between her shoulder blades. She arches her back and makes a contented noise in her throat.

'I just wanted you to know. How happy I am this morning. I knew it would be great, but I didn't expect it to be so...' She trails off and fixes him with those ridiculous, pale blue eyes. She bites her lip, and he bends to kiss where she's bitten.

'Earth-shattering? Life-changing? So much better than any other man you've ever been with?'

She shoves him. 'Insufferable. I didn't expect it to be so... emotionally charged. So intimate.'

She flicks her gaze away and back to him. He can tell this type of communication is difficult for her. The shower cubicle is a confessional, the roar of the water facilitating the baring of their souls.

'I know exactly what you mean.' His hands are on her jaw now, his thumbs holding her face up so she can find reassurance in his eyes. 'It was always going to be emotional for me, if I ever got to be with you, but I'm relieved I wasn't the only one feeling it.'

She turns away and busies herself with the shower gel, soaping up his stomach, over his chest and down his back to his backside, where she pauses. The soaping turns into a massage, and her face takes on a dreamy expression as she works. He watches her in amusement.

'I didn't know my arse was so dirty.'

'It's filthy. I need to be very thorough here.' Her expression regains some of its old archness, before her voice drops again. 'You weren't the only one feeling it, believe me. I was right there with you.'

'Even though I'm boring as hell?'

'Even though you're boring as hell. I'll admit, you have a few hidden talents.'

She nestles into him and stills, and he revels in the extraordinary experience of having the length of her naked body against his.

He scratches his fingernails lightly up and down her spine. 'You know, for two people who seem paranoid that the other one doesn't like their personality, we seem to have a pretty special connection.'

'Agreed,' she mumbles into his chest. Her ability to make eye contact during these admissions is severely limited, but he'll take it.

'So you're not going to run for the hills?' he persists. 'I'm not about to start 2019 broken-hearted?'

Her head shoots up. '*No*, Ned. No.Try getting rid of me.'

He's like a dog with a bone, but he needs to be sure. 'I thought you wouldn't be crazy about getting into another relationship, given you've just come out of a long one.'

'I have no problem with relationships.' Her arms are wrapped around him like a koala, and to her credit, she holds eye contact. 'I just don't want to be in a crappy one, and my last one had nothing to recommend it whatsoever. But when the guy in question is an absolute god'—she illustrates her point by running her hands down his back and squeezing his arse—'and as adorable and *fascinating* as you, it's another proposition entirely. I have no intention of letting you slip through my fingers.'

He smiles at *fascinating.* One final question. 'So, the test drive was to madam's liking?'

She pulls on his neck to bring his face down to hers. 'It was the ride of a lifetime,' she says into his mouth. 'Where do I sign?'

~

DAMP-HAIRED SADIE, sitting at his kitchen island in his fluffy grey robe, hugging a mug of her signature, over-brewed tea, is one of the most gratifying sights he's seen. The robe is huge on her, despite his best efforts to wrap her up tightly in it, and it slips off one shoulder. He abandons the avocado he's scooping out and shoots over, dropping a kiss on her delectable shoulder before she can adjust the robe.

'Why do you have two robes, anyway?' she teases. 'Do you have such high traffic of women coming through the house?'

'They're both mine. If I was smooth enough to have one for my conquests, I'd hopefully have been smooth enough to buy a smaller size.'

'But why two? I don't know anyone else who has two robes.'

'To rotate.' He resumes scooping out the flesh. 'I have a spare for when one's in the wash.'

She laughs.

'What?'

'Most people have one robe and they let it get disgustingly crusty and smelly and stained before they begrudgingly put it in the wash, and then they manage without it for a day or two while it's drying.'

He frowns. 'That's revolting. There's nothing nicer than a freshly laundered robe.'

She relents. 'Well, it's handy you have two. I'm very cosy. And we look cute, don't we? Matchy matchy.' She gestures to the chopping board. 'Like an advert for guacamole, or something. Instagram would love this moment.'

'Don't even think about it.'

'You don't like social media, do you?'

'Nope.'

'I know, because I tried stalking you. Couldn't find an account anywhere. I did find some old articles about the swim squad in the *Daily Princetonian*, though.' His jaw drops open, and her eyes take on a mischievous twinkle. 'What a little fish you were. And those budgie smugglers! Wowzers.'

Heat rises up his neck. 'You stalked me online?' For some reason this admission feels like the proof he's craved that she's been interested, these past few weeks.

'You bet I did. Once I'd seen you at the pool, I wanted to know more.'

'Have you any idea how shallow that makes you sound?' He laughs and looks up at her. 'Seriously, though. Are you telling me that's when you changed your opinion of me? When you saw me with my kit off? I would have stripped in the Monday meeting, if I'd known that was all it would take.'

'Kind of. Not really.' She's squirming now. 'And I'm not the only shallow one. You can't possibly have liked me for my personality.'

He's enjoying this. 'You're so right. Go on.'

'I admit, it did make me look at you with... new eyes, when I saw you virtually naked.'

He sniggers to himself as he chops coriander as finely as he can and adds it to the avocado flesh.

She bravely presses on. 'Not just because you have the most incredible body—'

'Why, thank you.' He blows her a kiss. 'It's all yours.'

'Mmm. Lucky, lucky me. But you were just—different, with your clothes off. I got a glimpse of the real you instead of the diaper-butt nerd you pretend to be at work.'

He's laughing openly now. '*What* did you call me?'

'Diaper-butt. It's a real thing; it refers to those chinos you wear that are so bulky around the bum that they make you look like you're wearing an adult nappy. It's a crime, if you ask me. You have a glorious bum; why wouldn't you show it off?'

He stares at her. 'I've never thought about it. My ex picked out most of those chinos for me.'

She points her teaspoon at him. 'Sabotage. She was trying to cover up your greatest assets so no one would notice your body at work. Evil. But highly effective. I'd never have guessed.'

'Wow.' He is amused. 'You'd better take me shopping, then. What should I be wearing at work?'

She rubs her hands in glee. 'This is going to be so much fun. I'm *nice* enough to share your body with the world. We'll go with fitted shirts and some well-tailored suit trousers to show off those snake hips. You're in good hands.'

'I don't doubt it. Well, thank the Lord I ran into you that day by the pool. Otherwise you'd still be ignoring me and my diaper-butt.'

'It wasn't really seeing you swimming that got me interested,' she says. 'I mean, it definitely sealed the deal. But it was the FT interview that made me realise I may have… overlooked you.'

'Really?' He looks up from his assembly line of toast, poached eggs and guacamole. 'That was a while ago.'

'Yup. I heard you in that interview and I realised I'd written you off as some deathly dull finance geek with a bad case of diaper butt.'

'Jesus.' He laughs and hands her a plate. 'Don't hold back, will you?'

She has the grace to look embarrassed. 'Sorry. Wow. This looks great, thanks. I just realised, when you were talking to Nithya, that you were actually pretty impressive and smart. It was sexy.'

'Oh, really.' He slides onto the bar stool next to her and pecks her on the cheek. '*Bon appétit*.'

'Yeah, really. It made me see you in a new light, in any case—I realised how dismissive I'd been of you.'

'You, dismissive? Never.' He raises an eyebrow as he tucks into his breakfast. The morning's exertions have made him ravenous. 'It makes sense, though. That was the only occasion I felt like you had any tolerance for me, when we chatted after the interview.'

She winces. 'Harsh but fair. Anyway, it was my loss. And then Nithya told me she was going to ask you out, and I was surprised by how weird that made me feel. And when she said you had a girlfriend, I was gutted. But I think I repressed it. Not good for my image, having a thing for diaper-butt guy.' She wiggles her eyebrows at him as she bites into a slice of toast. 'God, this is good. I'm starving.'

'And then…' he prompts. It's immensely gratifying, hearing her version of events when he's spent the past few weeks thinking she had no interest.

'And then I saw you in all your glory in the pool'—she gestures with her fork—'and I was sold. One hundred percent. I couldn't get you out of my head. But I thought you had a girlfriend, and I wasn't going to make the same mistake twice. So I've been completely, utterly miserable, and I've spent most of my energy trying and failing to get over you. And avoiding you like the plague. When you came up to me in the kitchen that day, and I was so rude to you... I knew how awful I'd been. I felt really bad. But it was that or jump you. I just had to get away from you. I couldn't even look at you—you blinded me too much.'

'I really wish you'd jumped me instead of trampling all over my heart. Those boots you had on—I can't tell you what they did to me. That little sliver of thigh between your dress and the top of the boots...' He shivers at the memory, and his face must look pretty intense, because he sees his own desire reflected back in her expression. He presses the point. 'You should wear them every day.'

'They're way too slutty for work. But if you invite me to stay tonight, I'll wear them for you. I'll go home and get them.'

'Easiest yes I've *ever* given.'

They beam at each other, the infinite promise of the weekend ahead glimmering between them. She takes a swig of tea.

'Thank God I took my tumble, and you came to my rescue.'

'Here's to you being drunk and clumsy.' He raises his coffee mug in a toast. 'How's the knee?' He nudges the hem of her robe open and takes a peek. The plaster is off and it's scabbing over.

'I'll live. And if I have a scar, I'll embrace it. It'll give me something to remember you by, if you cast me aside for a supermodel once we get you your fancy new work clothes.'

'You're not going to escape that easily.' He puts his free hand on her knee, palm up, and she takes it. He rubs her slim little hand with his thumb and watches her as she gazes around the room. She lets out a heavy sigh, and her shoulders drop.

'What's up?' he asks.

She looks at him and gathers herself together, and she purses her lips and lifts her head as if whatever she's going to say is intended to be a throwaway comment. 'You know, you shouldn't spoil me so much. Shower, robe, gourmet breakfast, perfectly brewed tea, *incredible* sex... I'll never want to leave.' Her eyes flick away from him.

He's got her number. There's more than an inkling of truth in her words, despite the characteristic quip in her tone. They have a long way to go to get to know each other in all the ways he wants to, but already he's horrified by the thought of her walking out through that door, when his bed will become just a bed again, his shower just a shower, his kitchen just a kitchen. When she's here, when he can touch her, these four walls hum with magic.

He puts down his mug, leans into her, and brushes her soft, sweet mouth with his. 'Then don't leave.'

EPILOGUE

Sunday, 27th January, 2019

'*Et voilà*.' Seb places a vast joint of beef on Belvedere's enormous kitchen table. Sadie can't quite believe *Seb Macleod* is cooking her Sunday lunch. Well, it's not really for her—it's in honour of Zoe, their new *Sunday Times Magazine* cover girl—but she's lucky enough to be invited along for the experience. The scent of perfectly cooked meat wafts around the table, and next to her, Ned groans theatrically.

'This looks *incredible*.'

The daily smitten gazes she gets from him have nothing on the love this piece of meat is getting right now. He's practically drooling. She laughs and puts her hand on his, and he drags his eyes away from the joint to smile at her. Relief: he still looks utterly lovesick as his eyes meet hers and he squeezes her hand tightly.

Seb's boyfriend, Gino, follows behind him, carrying a huge platter of roasted vegetables, glazed to perfection and dressed with mounds of fresh herbs, and Eddie brings up the rear, his steps deliberate and his eyes fixed firmly on the gravy boat wobbling ominously in his hands. Everyone cheers when it docks safely on the table.

Evelyn claps her hands. '*Bravo*. Spectacular, guys. *Thank you*.'

'My pleasure.' Seb wipes his hands down the front of his apron and picks up the carving knife and fork, holding them out to Angus. 'Does the host want to carve?'

'No way, mate.' Angus grins and holds up his hands. 'I'd botch it. I'll leave the carving to the pro, if you don't mind.'

Seb inclines his head, smiling in amusement. 'Certainly, sir.'

It's amazing to witness Evelyn's decidedly idyllic family life in action. Angus doesn't seem to mind Seb being here—the fact that his fiancée is sitting next to him, looking ravishing and wearing a totally lust-worthy diamond eternity ring on her left hand probably helps. Seb doesn't seem to mind the fact that Angus and Evelyn can't keep their hands off each other. He and Gino are pretty handsy too, come to think of it. In many ways, the fact that Seb is gay seems to be a simplifying factor. It removes so much of the awkwardness about them both moving on with other people. Sadie met Seb extremely briefly at the Sorrel Farm summer party last year, but she's far more tickled than she'd let on to be hanging out with him socially. It's clear why he's such achieved such celebrity status: he's obscenely good-looking in the flesh and has an easy charm that makes everyone bask in the glow of his attention. Gino is absolutely gorgeous, too. Surely some fabulous menswear brand will pick them up as models soon. She could definitely see them doing a Dolce and Gabbana ad campaign.

Evelyn looks positively ecstatic to have her whole

extended family around her. The woman of the hour, Zoe, smiles her usual beatific smile next to her hilarious wife. Their kids, Mike and Mia, are weirdly well-behaved and delightful. Little Eddie is ecstatic to have both his parents and their other halves in the same room. Kudos to Seb and Evelyn; they seem to have handled the whole divorce brilliantly, and Eddie gets on famously with both Angus and Gino. It's apparent that Angus is a very loving, stable influence in his life whereas Gino and Eddie have a more frat-boy relationship; there's a lot of guffawing and high-fiving between them.

Angus' sons, Hector and Alastair, are here too. Angus hinted earlier that they were less interested in celebrating Alastair's godmother, Zoe, than in upgrading their usual uni beans on toast to Sunday lunch cooked by a world-famous chef. Sadie's thrilled that she and Ned were included. Evelyn was kind enough to tell her she wanted to include them as a thank you to Sadie for securing the feature on Zoe, but really she suspects it's so Evelyn can observe, and obsess over, her and Ned together and unleashed from the usual confines of having to behave professionally. Evelyn could not have been more excited when Sadie spilled the beans about Ned. You'd think she'd orchestrated the whole thing herself.

They're all ecstatic, to be fair. It's clear Ned is the golden boy where Angus, Evelyn, Jess and Zoe are concerned. They've all given her smiling but thinly veiled warnings not to fuck him over. They needn't worry. She's so addicted to him that she feels like she's on narcotics most of the time. She sneaks a look at him; he looks so handsome in his shirt and cashmere sweater, his hair falling over his eyes in that way she loves so much. He's still holding her hand, and he absent-mindedly rubs his thumb back and forth over her knuckles. She feels a rush of love and pride that warms her groin as much as her heart. Just being able to sit next to him, and enjoy his gorgeous looks and his wonderful Ned-ness, and know that she's his, is almost too much. She hasn't told him she loves him yet—they've only been together a month —but she can't keep it in much longer. Her need to share her feelings with him is bursting out of her.

She takes a slug of her claret while Seb carves. She likes her wines, but this is another level, its earthiness perfectly balanced by the smooth silkiness with which it slips down.

'Oh my lord,' she says. 'This wine is incredible!'

'Thank Seb.' Angus gestures with his head. 'I only proposed to Evelyn because Seb agreed to give her some of the wine cellar in the divorce settlement.'

'It was worth it to get her off my hands,' Seb quips.

'Hilarious.' Evelyn makes a face at them both. 'Actually, Angus and I had our first—moment—together after getting somewhat over-served on Seb's claret last summer, didn't we, darling?'

'We certainly did.' Angus smiles at her in a way that must make Evelyn weak at the knees. They really are adorable together. 'I'd never have dared hope that we'd all be sitting together like this, a few months later, in our beautiful home, with everyone loved-up and happy, and our kids thriving. How did we get so lucky?'

There's a misty-eyed silence for a moment around the table until Hector or Alastair—she's not sure which is which —pipes up: *Get it together, Dad, for Christ's sake*, and everyone laughs.

When Seb has served up, Evelyn gets gracefully to her feet.

'I don't want to get between you and Seb's cooking. I just

want to say congratulations to our amazing Zoe. You've done us proud and I know for a fact that this is just the beginning of a very exciting journey for you, and for our farm. And well done Sadie for pulling this interview out of the bag. I told you this was my dream, and you nailed it. I'm so happy to have you all here. I love every one of you, even my ex-husband. Thanks, Seb, for trekking down here and spoiling us all. Now, eat up.'

~

Later that afternoon, Ned sits on his sofa with Sadie in front of the fire. They're both sprawled out to give their swollen stomachs as much space as possible, and Sadie's abandoned the belt she was wearing over her beautiful, floaty black dress. He rubs her stomach gently, and she groans.

'Why did I have a second helping of sticky toffee pudding?'

'Because when a world-famous chef agrees to abandon his healthy-eating brand strategy for long enough to serve up the mother of all Sunday lunches, we tuck in.'

'Mmm.'

She doesn't seem capable of much conversation. She swings herself around and lowers her head onto his lap. At the sight of her gazing up at him, her beautiful golden hair a halo around her, he can barely speak himself. She smiles at him and her dimples come out to say hello. He'll never get used to that sight. Her hand is on her own, quite impressively distended, stomach now, rubbing it lightly. It transports him to a place that he almost daren't think of, a place where one day she's expecting his baby and she lies on the sofa, just like this, as she grows it. He needs to distract himself.

'Let me take another look at my clever girlfriend's handiwork.' He strokes her hair before picking up the *Sunday Times Magazine* from the top of the pile of supplements next to him. Sadie has surpassed herself. They've gone with a shot of Zoe in the kitchen. The lighting is moody, just bright enough to pick up the lustre of the copper pans hanging above her. Her hands, in oven mitts, embrace what looks like a delicious gratin of some sort, and the surrounding surface is adorned with brightly coloured vegetables. She's radiant and beautiful. The journalist has gone with the headline she'd tipped Sadie off about: *Heaven on Earth. Sorrel Farm's Head Chef, Zoe Augustin, shows us how to find connection with each other and our planet through our plates.*

They've both read the article at least three times already, but he flips through it again before putting the magazine aside. Stroking Sadie's hair is far more enjoyable.

'You're so amazing,' he tells her. His fingers start at her temples and slide through her glossy golden locks. She arches her back at his touch and sighs. Those ridiculous pale blue eyes are fixed on him in a way that he knows, from blessed experience, bode well for him later. He sits, and enjoys the weight of her head in his lap, and runs his fingers through her hair, and thinks that he's never felt happier in his life. She went home for Christmas Day and Boxing Day, as did he, and they both raced back to Sevenoaks on the twenty-seventh, desperate to see each other. She hasn't spent a night at her own place since. Come to think of it, that was exactly a month ago. He's going to suggest she jack in her pointless rental and move in here officially. It's a waste of her money to hold on to it, and he doesn't want to spend a night away from her.

It's been amazing, working with her, seeing her every day, coming home to her every evening. He's had to employ every ounce of discipline learnt in his years of swim squad to keep his head on his job when he's at work. She took him shopping in the Christmas sales and got him kitted out with new fitted shirts and slim-cut chinos. He likes them perfectly well, but he *loves* the effect they have on her. She'd be all over him all day, if it was remotely appropriate. They've both ramped up their poolside meets, and they've even had to, very discreetly, avail of the disabled changing room a couple of times when they've wound each other up too much in the pool. He doesn't know who this new version of himself is, but she seems into him, and that's all he cares about.

She turns her head and hauls herself upright before clambering over his lap so she's straddling him. Her lips brush his and he breathes her in.

'Hello, you,' she says.

'Hello, *you*.'

'I have to tell you something.' She's stroking his face now, his hair.

'What's up?'

'Nothing's up. But I wanted to tell you I love you.' She stares at him before burying her face in his neck, and he puts his arms around her and squeezes her as tightly as he can. His heart is pounding and he can scarcely believe she's just uttered the words he's dreamt of hearing for as long as he's known her.

'Hey.' He loosens his grip and eases her away so he can see her. 'Honey. I love you too. I've been wanting to say it for ages, but I didn't want to freak you out.' He smiles at her and watches to make sure she understands what he's saying.

'Really?' She shifts forward in his lap, and he groans inwardly at the heavenly sensation. 'I love you so much,' she tells him. 'So much, I don't know what to do with myself. I'm a mess.'

'You don't need to be a mess. You've made my dream come true; I'm just sorry you beat me to it. I didn't want to freak you out by saying anything too soon, but this is it for me. I'm yours forever, if you want me.'

She gives him a smile full of wonder. 'How long have you wanted to say it for?'

'Well.' He considers. 'I fell for you the first time I saw you. I was besotted from word go; you know that. And I've been wanting to say it for the past month. But if I'm honest, what I feel now is so much more than what I felt then. Now that I know the real you, and I get to be close to you in all the most amazing ways, I love you so much more. I just can't believe I get to plan a future with you.'

Her face is soft. She's never looked so tender or undone.

'You *are* my future.' She pushes him gently in the chest, and his fingers lace behind her back. 'I hope you know that.'

Her mouth is on his now, and he kisses her as gently and deliberately as he can. Because even if they have a future together, he doesn't want to let this moment, or any moment with her, slip by without committing it to memory. It feels fresh every time he kisses her: the satiny slide of her lips, the softness of her tongue as it meets his. He can feel her trembling slightly before she pulls away.

'I mean to say,' she continues, 'my future is you and any nerdy little offspring we may happen to produce along the way.' The nonchalant shrug she gives him doesn't fool him for a second, and his heart thumps under her hand.

'I think your brattish genes will overpower my nerdy ones.' He matches the playfulness of her tone, but their eyes tell a different story. Hers are shining.

'I hope we don't have a girl,' he says. He could drown in

these eyes. 'She'll be a total blue-eyed diva, and she'll have me completely in her clutches. Exactly like her mother. I won't stand a chance.'

She smiles at him, sweetly, angelically, before whispering so softly in his ear that his neck breaks out in goosebumps. 'You'll be screwed.'

WHEN THEN BECOMES NOW

You're seventeen, and you're hopelessly, crazily in love.

One night, everything goes tragically wrong, and you won't see him for twenty-one long years.

When your paths cross again, you're married. And he's famous.

How can you be together? How can you *not*?

ABOUT ME

I like to change things up! I spent my 20s as a banker and my 30s bringing up small children and running my own fashion brand (Madderson London).

I started writing aged 41, and I wonder why I didn't do it sooner.

I've always loved writing. My daughter Tilly has an old notebook of mine filled with half-finished stories and accompanying drawings. I've read for as long as I can remember, guzzling up books so quickly that my mum always protested that I couldn't be reading them properly.

I published my first book, *Metamorphosis*, in February 2020, right before lockdown happened. It's a non-fiction book about escaping from our cocoons and living as a butterfly. As lockdown progressed, I found escapism in devouring lots of delicious chick-lit (for want of a better title) and I realised I had a few novels in me too. I have loved every single minute of writing them.

I've published my books independently, and I love the freedom it provides. The world of independent publishing is fascinating and so empowering--I'm delighted to share more of my experiences of self-publishing if you're interested.

I'd love to hear from you with feedback, suggestions and requests! My email is sara@saramadderson.com.

facebook.com/saramaddersonauthor
twitter.com/saramadderson
instagram.com/saramaddersonauthor

ALSO BY SARA MADDERSON

FICTION

Food for Thought (1st in the Sorrel Farm series)

Parents & Teachers

The Winter's Fail

NON-FICTION

Metamorphosis

Printed in Great Britain
by Amazon

65245164R00149